"You're a terrible actress," Jack replied, far too easily.

He squatted in front of her chair, still caging her between his strong arms, but now his muscled thighs spread open before her and his face—his mouth—was much too close to hers. She dared not move. He was so big, so male, and as dangerous as he was compelling. She wanted to leap out of the chair and run screaming from the room—the inn—the island. But more than that, she wanted to lean forward and touch him. Both propositions were terrifying.

"Why don't you just admit what you came for?" His voice was insinuating.

Larissa sucked in a deep breath. And then, because she knew that he would never believe her, that he saw only what he wanted to see—only what she'd worked so hard to show to the world for so long, and never anything else, never anything beneath that mask—she told him the truth.

"I had no idea you'd be here," she said quietly.

Scandal in the Spotlight

The truth is more shocking than the headline!

Named and most definitely shamed,
these media darlings have learned the hard way
that the press always loves a scandal!

Having a devastatingly gorgeous man on their arm only
adds fuel to the media frenzy. Especially when
the attraction between them burns hotter and brighter
than a paparazzi's flashbulb…

Look out for BACK IN THE HEADLINES
by Sharon Kendrick in December!

If you missed Michelle Conder's
GIRL BEHIND THE SCANDALOUS REPUTATION
in May—don't forget it's available in eBook!

Caitlin Crews

HEIRESS BEHIND THE HEADLINES

HARLEQUIN®
entertain, enrich, inspire™

Recycling programs
for this product may
not exist in your area.

ISBN-13: 978-0-373-23861-3

HEIRESS BEHIND THE HEADLINES

First North American Publication 2012

www.Harlequin.com

Printed in U.S.A.

All about the author...
Caitlin Crews

CAITLIN CREWS discovered her first romance novel at the age of twelve. It involved swashbuckling pirates, grand adventures, a heroine with rustling skirts and a mind of her own, and a seriously mouthwatering and masterful hero. The book (the title of which remains lost in the mists of time) made a serious impression. Caitlin was immediately smitten with romances and romance heroes, to the detriment of her middle school social life. And so began her lifelong love affair with romance novels, many of which she insists on keeping near her at all times.

Caitlin has made her home in places as far-flung as York, England, and Atlanta, Georgia. She was raised near New York City, and fell in love with London on her first visit when was a teenager. She has backpacked in Zimbabwe, been on safari in Botswana and visited tiny villages in Namibia. She has, while visiting the place in question, declared her intention to live in Prague, Dublin, Paris, Athens, Nice, the Greek Islands, Rome, Venice and/or any of the Hawaiian islands. Writing about exotic places seems like the next best thing to moving there.

She currently lives in California with her animator/comic-book-artist husband and their menagerie of ridiculous animals.

Other titles by Caitlin Crews available in eBook:

Harlequin Presents®

CHAPTER ONE

LARISSA Whitney's luck ran out with the loud thump of the heavy door that let in the howl and clamor of the wet November winds outside, shaking the rain-soaked windows in front of her.

She looked away from the gray, brooding Atlantic waves that crashed against the rocky shore of the isolated Maine island, glancing without particular interest toward the door of the tiny restaurant that was also the only bar in the only inn on the only stretch of desolate road that could be called a village in this place, so far from the blue skies and sunny days of the summer high season. So far from anywhere—which was why she'd come. She'd expected nothing but the near-total isolation she'd been seeking, and for the past few days, that was exactly what she'd found.

So, naturally, *he* walked in.

Her stomach dropped with a thud as she took in the man at the door. She blinked, as if he was an apparition and she could banish him back into the depths of her memory that way, but no: Jack Endicott Sutton was still shouldering his way inside, shaking off the weather as he peeled the battered rain jacket from his long, lean frame and hung it on the coatrack.

"Anyone but Jack Sutton…" Larissa whispered to herself, not meaning to speak aloud. Her fingers clenched hard around the mug of coffee she'd been nursing while she brooded about the mess of her life. "Please…" But there was no one listening, and it was no use anyway.

It was him. It could hardly be anyone else.

She recognized him instantly, as she imagined everybody on the planet in possession of two working eyes would. That surprisingly beautiful, richly masculine face was burned into her mind, as familiar to her as that of any major movie star in any glossy magazine, which he'd certainly spent enough time adorning in his day. More familiar to her, perhaps, because she knew him personally. That long, leanly muscled body was famous for the Yale rugby shirt he'd worn as an undergraduate, the Harvard Law gravitas that was said to infuse it later, and, of course, the many beautiful women, starlets and models and socialites without number, that usually clung to it.

Tonight—or was it late afternoon? It was hard to tell the difference so far north—Jack wore a simple black, long-sleeved T-shirt that clung to his celebrated torso over a pair of weathered old jeans that made his lean hips and strong legs into a kind of powerful male poetry, and a pair of what looked to her like incongruous workman's boots. He should have looked as if he was playing dress up, when she knew that he more commonly viewed Armani as casual wear when he was in his usual element, glittering brightly in the midst of the Manhattan high life. Barring that, he should have blended right in with the other locals who had wandered in while Larissa had nursed her hot coffee in the farthest corner, all of them dressed just as he was—but he didn't.

She doubted Jack Sutton had ever *blended* in his life. And it made her heart kick against the walls of her chest. Hard.

Centuries of blood so blue it shone like sapphires coursed in his veins, making him far more than just a shockingly good-looking man with rich dark hair and dark chocolate eyes—though he was certainly that. He wore the whole of his family's great and glorious history with complete nonchalance, like a mighty weapon he didn't need to brandish. All those noble Boston Brahmins and lofty Knickerbocker families of Gilded Age Manhattan who peppered his ancestry were evident in the easy way he moved, the power and pure arrogance that emanated from him, as much a part of him as the long, strong lines of the body some regarded as a national treasure. Jack's hallowed ancestors were all of them captains of industry, leaders and visionaries, kings of philanthropy and canny investors. And he was every inch their heir. Every last muscled, beautiful, proud and dangerous inch.

She knew who he was, where he came from. She came from the same lofty heights, for all her sins. But Larissa knew what else he was: her absolute worst nightmare. And he was blocking her only escape route.

Nice job, Larissa, she told herself, veering somewhere between despair and a kind of bitterness that felt too much like anticipation. *You can't even disappear to the ends of the earth properly.*

But there was no point getting hysterical. She slumped down in her seat, and pulled the hooded sweater tighter around her, as if the thick gray wool might camouflage her somehow. As if she could disappear into it the way she'd wanted to disappear from the face of the earth—or at least, from everything she knew. Her "life," such as it was.

She forced herself to look away from the compelling figure of Manhattan's Most Eligible Bachelor, back out to the sea, where the merciless waves beat at the craggy coastline, inexorable and fierce. He probably wouldn't even recognize her, she told herself. She had left New York months ago and had told no one where she was going. And anyway, she was hardly known for spending time in near-abandoned places like this godforsaken island, a million miles from the nearest five-star spa without so much as lip gloss on her face, wearing nothing but jeans and a sweater that could double as a cloak. Not to mention, she'd cut off all her trademark blond tresses before she'd left and dyed what remained of it black for exactly this reason—to avoid being recognized, even by the people who had known her in her long and complicated former life.

Even by ghosts of weekends past, like Jack Sutton, who, she had the uncomfortable feeling, was not the sort of person who was easily fooled. Not even by someone like Larissa, who had been fooling everyone around her for years. Hadn't she discovered that firsthand? Wasn't that why the very fact that he was here, in this smaller-by-the-moment restaurant and bar, made her so tense, suddenly? So…wound up?

She ordered herself to breathe, just the way the doctors had taught her to do back in New York. *Breathe.* He wouldn't even notice her, and if he did, he certainly wouldn't realize that she was—

"Larissa Whitney."

His voice was cool and low, just this side of amused. It moved over her skin like a caress, then moved inside, making her feel as though she was shaking to pieces when she knew she wasn't moving at all.

Breathe.

But she suspected that was out of the question.

He didn't wait for an invitation, he simply threw himself into the chair opposite hers, his dark brown eyes gleaming with something she was afraid to identify when she finally dared meet his gaze. His long legs stretched out before him, crowding her under the small table, and she couldn't help but move hers out of the way. She hated herself for even so slight an indication of weakness, so small an acknowledgment that he got under her skin. Damn him.

Why did it have to be Jack Sutton, of all people? What was he even doing here? He was the one person she'd never quite managed to mislead, not even when he'd been as lost a cause as she was. Why did it have to be him? It had been months since anyone had even known her name, and now she was trapped on an inhospitable island with a man who knew too much. He always had. It was only one of the reasons he was so formidable. So dangerous to her health.

She had the sudden, insane urge to pretend she didn't recognize him. To pretend she was someone else. *I have no idea who Larissa Whitney is,* she could say, and it wouldn't even really be a lie, would it? She could simply deny her own existence, and maybe, just maybe, escape the great weight of it that way. Part of her wanted to, with a ferocity that should not have shocked her.

But he was looking at her with those too-knowing eyes of his, and she didn't dare.

She smiled instead, the perfunctory sort of public smile she had perfected in the cradle. She'd been well into her teens before someone had pointed out to her that smiles were supposed to reach the eyes. She'd been skeptical.

"Guilty as charged," she said, keeping her voice light, easy. Unbothered. Unaffected by this man, by the sizzling shock of his proximity, of her unexpected response to him—so strong and male and *alive*. She shifted in her seat, but kept her face smooth. Empty. Just as he'd expect it to be. Just as she worried she truly was.

"So I hear." He smirked, his eyes never leaving hers, the challenge unmistakable. Or was that a cool dose of contempt? She could hardly tell the difference these days. "I didn't see any paparazzi swarming over the village like ants. No yachts cluttering up the bay in the middle of a November storm. No clubs heaving with the rich and the terminally bored. Did you somehow mistake the coast of Maine for the south of France?"

"It's wonderful to see you, too," she murmured, as if that scathing, judgmental tone didn't bother her. And why should it? She should have been well-used to it by now, having heard nothing but her whole life. Having, in fact, gone out of her way to court it from all and sundry. "How long has it been? Five years? Six?"

"What are you doing here, Larissa?" he asked, and his voice was not nice. Not polite. This from a man who could charm anyone he pleased—who had been doing so the whole of his privileged life. She knew. She'd seen him in action. She'd experienced exactly how powerfully charming he could be. She repressed a shiver.

"Can't a girl take a little vacation?" she asked idly. Playfully. As if she felt either. But she knew better than to show him anything else.

"Not here." His cool eyes narrowed slightly as he watched her, and she pretended she couldn't feel her own reaction to him, unfolding inside of her. Wariness, she told herself—that's all it was. But she knew better. "There's nothing here for you. One general store. This inn. Less than fifty families. That's it. There are only two ferries to the mainland a week—and that's weather permitting." His perfect mouth firmed into a grim line. "There's absolutely no reason in the world someone like you should be here."

"It's the hospitality," she said dryly, nodding at him as if he'd welcomed her with a song and open arms. "It's addictive."

She leaned back in her chair, not sure why her

stomach knotted, why her limbs felt weak and traitorous. She'd known Jack all her life. They'd been
raised in the same glittering, claustrophobic circles
of New York City's very, very wealthy. The same
elite private schools, the same Ivy League expectations. The same attractive and well-maintained
faces at all the same parties, in places like Aspen,
the Hamptons, Miami and Martha's Vineyard.

She remembered being a teenager and running
into Jack, then in his resplendent twenties, at some
desperately chic party one summer. She could still
imagine him as he'd been then, golden and gleaming on a private beach in the Hamptons, seeming
to outshine the very sun above him. He'd been
loose-limbed and easygoing, with a killer smile
and that devastating intellect beneath. Everyone
she'd known had been desperately in love with
him. When she thought of Jack Sutton, that was
always how she remembered him. Bright. Ines-
capably beautiful. All summer in his smile.

But there was no sign of that young man here,
now. And she had other memories she'd rather
not excavate. The ones from that one weekend
she preferred to block out. The ones that featured
him a little bit older, and a whole lot more shattering than she cared to remember in any detail. The
ones that made it clear that whatever else he was,
he was distinctly dangerous to her, personally. All

that heat. All that fire. And eyes like bittersweet, decadent chocolate that saw too much, too deep.

The truth was that this man had fascinated her and then terrified her. And all of that was before. *Before*. Before she'd had her own little resurrection, her own second chance. At what, she might not know. But she did know that the arrival of Jack Sutton was like throwing a bomb into the middle of it. He was uncontrollable. Impossible. And those were two of his better qualities.

She settled back in her chair, assuming the careless, languid sort of position that came to her so easily, like a second skin. The usual Larissa Whitney insouciance she could summon at will, automatically adjusting to his assumptions, to what he no doubt already saw when he looked at her. She was so good at living down to the world's expectations. She sometimes wondered if it was her only true skill.

"Are you in disguise?" he continued, in that same lethally soft voice that made the fine hairs on the back of her neck rise. His cool brown gaze flicked over her, made her want to squirm. But she only lounged, making herself look like the very essence of boredom. "Or on the run? Do I even want to know what fantasy you're playing at here?"

"Why are you so interested?" she asked, letting

out a light sort of laugh. "Are you afraid it doesn't include you?"

"Quite the opposite." His tone was curt, his eyes hard. As if she'd done something to him, personally. She blinked, taken aback. She certainly could have, of course. She just thought she'd remember it. Jack Sutton wasn't the sort of man anyone forgot. Repressed, yes. Forgot? Never.

"I heard Maine is lovely this time of year," she said, forestalling whatever character assassination he might be about to unleash on her. She wasn't certain she could survive it—not from him. It made her stomach ache just to look at him. "How could I resist?"

She nodded toward the window, inviting him to do the same. The sky had darkened, the clouds moving fast against the swollen pewter clouds. Rain beat at the glass, while below, the rocks withstood the angry assault of the waves. She felt like those rocks, battered and beleaguered, yet somehow still standing—with her own past the tragic, inescapable crash of the sea. Jack, she thought, was just the rain. A cold, depressing insult on top of a far greater injury.

"You've had a banner year already, haven't you," Jack said, in that way. That knowing way. "Or so I hear."

It made her feel horribly exposed, naked and vulnerable—things she strove to avoid at all costs,

especially around this man, after the last time—
and the worst part was that she couldn't even tell
him the real story. She couldn't defend herself.
She had to accept the fiction—and worse, the fact
that everyone so easily believed that the fiction
was truth. Why did it hurt so much this time?
It was no different than any other scandal, was
it? It was only that this time around, the fiction
wasn't of her own making.

"Oh, yes," Larissa agreed, hating him. Hating
herself more. "A little tour of duty in rehab, a silly
little broken engagement. Thanks so much for reminding me." What could she say? *That wasn't
me. I was in a coma, and there was a woman
who masqueraded as me, who ended up with my
fiancé...* Hardly. Her life was enough of a soap
opera without all the gory, patently unbelievable
details.

After all, the entire world knew that Larissa
Whitney, famous for being nothing more than a
worthless party girl and a great embarrassment
to her storied family, had collapsed outside of an
elite Manhattan club one night some eight months
ago. Thanks to the endless scrutiny of the tabloids—and the usual manipulations her media-
savvy family was so well versed in—the world
also knew what had happened next. Larissa had
been packed away to a private rehabilitation center for a while, then paraded around Manhattan

on the arm of her long-suffering fiancé, Theo, the CEO of her family's company. Until Theo had left Larissa and—more shocking by far, given his well-documented ambitions—Whitney Media behind. Everyone blamed faithless, heartless Larissa. And why not? She'd gone out of her way to hurt Theo as publicly and as repeatedly as possible. For years. She was the obvious villain.

The fact that she had never been in rehab—and that she'd been hidden away for two months in a hospital bed in the family mansion, expected to die while her family engaged in their usual cruel machinations over her comatose body—well, that wasn't nearly as interesting a story, was it? Not nearly as familiar, as expected.

But he wouldn't believe her anyway. No one would. And she had no one to blame for that but herself, as usual.

"Haven't you caused enough trouble?" Jack asked then, as if he'd read her mind. She believed that if anyone could, it was Jack, and the thought made that shiver roll through her again. He shook his head slightly, as if she wearied him unto his soul. "Do you think you're going to drag me into one of your messes? You might want to think again, Larissa. I stopped playing your kind of games a long time ago."

"If you say so," she said, as if she was bored. As if she was not even now struggling to keep herself from jumping to her feet and bolting for the door. Anything to get away from that awful, judgmental look in his eyes—eyes that seemed to look deep into her and see nothing but her darkest secrets. Her shame.

God, she hated him.

But she'd rather die than show him that he'd hurt her. She certainly couldn't tell him why she was really here, on a pine-studded scrap of land eight miles out from Bar Harbor, in the middle of the lashing wind with only the desolate sea in every direction. She couldn't tell him she'd ended up on the ferry because she'd been trying so hard to disappear for months now, to really be as invisible as she felt—she wouldn't even know how to say those things. Or to explain how she felt about this miraculous second chance she'd been given at a life she'd ruined so thoroughly, treated so carelessly, the first go-round. And certainly not to Jack, whom she still thought of as bright and shining and untouchable, no matter the dark, hard look he was training on her now. No matter the power and command he seemed to wear like a second skin.

She had promised herself that she would never lie to herself, not ever again, and she meant to keep that promise. But that didn't mean she owed him the same courtesy. And there was so little of her left, so little of her she could even identify as her own, and she knew, somehow, that if she gave him even a tiny bit of that he could crush her forever. She just knew.

So she gave him what he wanted. What he already saw. She smiled at him, the mysterious, closemouthed smile she'd learned to give the press a long time ago—the smile that made men crazy, that exuded sex, that made everyone project all their fantasies and wishes and dreams onto her while she simply stood there and was empty. Nothing. Just a screen.

She was good at that, too.

She cocked her head to the side, and met his gaze as if his words had rolled right off her, as if they were nothing at all. As if this was nothing but a flirtation, some delicious kind of foreplay they were both engaging in. She let her brows rise, let her lips part suggestively. She made her voice low, sexy. The expected fantasy. She could produce it by rote, and no one ever suspected a thing.

"Tell me more, Jack," she purred. "What kind of games do you like to play?"

CHAPTER TWO

SHE looked so fragile. Those delicate, perfect cheekbones that had announced her identity from across the room, even when he'd been unable to imagine what a creature like her, better used to lounging about in Manhattan's most elite circles surrounded by sycophants and other fashionably bored and useless socialites, could possibly be doing in a place as remote as this island. Those mysterious, always-sad eyes of a haunted, storm-tossed green that hinted at depths she would never, could never, possess.

That was the great lie of Larissa Whitney, he thought with no little distaste—almost aimed more at himself for his susceptibility to that lie than at her for perpetuating it. Almost.

Because he could still feel that maddening electricity crackle through him, though he'd spent a long time denying it had ever existed. Yet it had jolted through him anyway, unmistakable and unwelcome, when he'd looked across the bar and seen her sitting there, looking…oddly bereft.

It roared back through him now, as she flirted with him, her lush lips parting slightly as she ran a deliberate finger along the lower one. Tempting him. Luring him. Making him think back to the sweet perfection of her legs wrapped tightly around his hips. The taste of that perfect, wicked mouth. But he was no longer the kind of man who bowed down to his appetites, especially when they were as self-destructive as this one. Especially when he knew exactly how little a woman like Larissa had to offer to a man in his position, a man who preferred to think about his reputation before his pleasure these days. And her reputation was about as black and dire as they came.

"Nice try," he said dismissively, as if his body wasn't hard and ready just looking at her. Not that he would let that matter. "But one taste of that was more than enough."

He thought he saw something move through her green eyes then, but it was gone with a blink, and she only smiled at him. That dangerous, mysterious smile of hers, like a siren's song, that tempted him to forget all he knew. That tempted him to simply lean forward, put his hands on her lush little body, yank her mouth to his, and taste her.

"Oh, Jack," she murmured, her voice little more than a purr, the timbre of it seeming to pool in his groin, then light a path of fire across his skin. "That's what they all say. At first."

He wished she wasn't so good at this. He wished he wasn't so affected. He wished he could look at her and see what he knew to be the truth of her— instead of that elegant, vulnerable line of her neck, the exposed turn of her delicate jaw, that made him want to comfort her, however insane that urge was. He wished that the short, inky-black hair did not suit her so much more than it should have. It made her seem more serious, more substantial.

But he knew better. He knew what she was. What she'd done. Every dirty detail. He knew everything there was to know about her, and it didn't matter how small or helpless she might appear on the surface. He knew that she was soulless beneath. Like all the rest of them in that world he'd left behind. Just like he had been, before he'd grown up.

Looking at her was like looking into a mirror he'd deliberately broken five years ago, and he disliked what he saw. He always would. And she'd been the one to hold that mirror up to him in the first place. How could he ever forget that?

"There will be a ferry leaving at dawn on Friday," he said coldly, abruptly, his voice showing none of the roughness within. "I want you on it."

She laughed. It was a silvery sound, magical.

It made him wish for things that he knew better than to believe in, and he blamed her for that, too.

"Are you ordering me off this island?" she asked, looking delighted at the prospect. And not in the least bit intimidated by him, which, it hurt him to admit, he found more attractive than he should. "How dictatorial. I might swoon."

Jack eyed her. This was his refuge. His escape. He hid here in the dark, grim winter months when none of the well-heeled tourists and summer residents were around—New England's and Manhattan's oldest money in their ancient family homes and compounds, cluttering up the island and hoarding all the summer sunshine for themselves as if it was their rightful due. He preferred it here now, in these forgotten months, when he didn't have to be *Jack Endicott Sutton,* too-eligible heir to two magnificent American fortunes, and yet still the bane of his grandfather's august existence. Here, he did not have to think about his duty. Here, he could breathe without worrying how each exhalation reflected on his suitability to manage the Endicott Foundation, his family's prominent charitable foundation. Here, tucked away in the worst of the unforgiving Maine weather, shoulder to shoulder with lobstermen and fishermen who respected only the sea—and only sometimes at that—he was just Jack.

He couldn't have Larissa Whitney polluting this

place, playing God only knew what kind of games in the closest thing he had to a sanctuary. It was unthinkable. And he suspected he could guess what she was doing so far from her preferred glittering, high-end stomping grounds. Down east Maine in the off-season, subject to the treacherous weather and notably bereft of breathless page-six gossip, was no place for a spoiled, pampered, overly indulged party girl. There were no parties here. No press. No screaming, adoring masses on every corner, ready to copy her clothes and sell her secrets to the highest bidder. None of the things someone like Larissa considered basics for survival. He was afraid he could guess what had brought her here, and he didn't like it at all.

"You haven't bothered to ask what I'm doing here," he pointed out, searching the smooth mask of her beautiful face, so adored by so many, for clues, but of course, there was nothing there. There never was. Nothing she didn't want him to see. Nothing to see at all, he thought. He was annoyed that he even looked for anything more. "Is that your usual self-absorption, or did you expect to see me when you got here?"

"You tossed open the door like a modern-day Heathcliff," she murmured, as if transported into rapturous daydreams by the very idea. He didn't believe her for a moment. Like all of her peers, all saddled with names that dated back to the origin of the country, and to the lauded coal, steel and robber-baron fortunes that had built it, she could be a fantastic actress when it suited her. But could she be anything else? And why did he still want to know?

"It's all very romantic," she said when he only gazed at her. She shrugged. "I'd hate all the gritty little travel details—your itinerary, my schedule, so boring—to ruin such a delicious moment."

"I think I know why you're here," he said, ignoring her flirtatious little performance. Her games might have worked on him once, he told himself, but they wouldn't again. His voice lowered. "Did you really think this would work, Larissa? Have you forgotten that I know how you operate?"

She blinked, and he had the impression that for that moment, she truly had no idea what he meant. But then he reminded himself that this—precisely this—was what she was best at.

She leaned forward then, putting her hand high on his thigh and letting her body sway toward his and, *no,* Jack thought. He'd been wrong. *This* was what she was best at. This effortless seduction. With just a touch, using only her proximity. She was irresistible and she knew it. *Lethal.*

So close, her unique fragrance seemed to fill his head, spinning it—a hint of unusual, expensive spices, edgy and intriguing. And the cream of her skin was scented a warm, intoxicating vanilla. He remembered far more than he wanted to, more than he was comfortable admitting even to himself. Her taste, her scent. The wild passion that he'd long since decided he'd imagined, embellished. But there was no imagining this. Her hand burned through his jeans, searing into his flesh, stirring him, reminding him exactly how much he'd wanted her—and still did. But that didn't mean he had to give into it. Or even like it. Or her.

He stood, watching her hand fall away. Part of him wanted to reach out and put his own hands on her, all over her. Relearn her curves, her cries. Lose himself in her.

But he was no longer that man. He'd graduated from the kind of games Larissa played five years ago, and he wasn't going back.

"Friday," he said, his voice commanding. Sure of her instant obedience. "The ferry. Six-thirty in the morning. It's not a request."

"I appreciate the update on the ferry schedule," she said evenly. Once again, he saw something he didn't understand in her green gaze—something that didn't make sense. She didn't look away, and he found he couldn't decipher her. And surely, she should be an open book, made up of blank pages, shouldn't she? "But I'll do what I want, Jack. Not what you tell me to do."

"Not on this island, you won't." He could feel

the ferocity of his smile. He was enjoying this too much, suddenly.

Her elegant brows rose, and that smile of hers sharpened. "I hate to point out the obvious to a person whose relatives were on hand to sign the Declaration of Independence and carry on afterward in the streets of Philadelphia," she drawled, her eyes flashing. "But it remains a free country."

"Except on this island," he said. And smiled wider, arrogant and proud. "I own it."

She was such an idiot.

There was no getting around it, Larissa thought when she was tucked away in her tiny attic room in the inn, neck-deep in the claw-footed tub that she suspected had been there since the 1800s. *Endicott Island.* She should have known. It was right there in his name.

Although, in her defense, she knew a great many people whose family names were littered about the country—on streets, towns, buildings, bridges. Her own, for example. That didn't necessarily translate into members of that family appearing wherever they were named, as if called forth by some spell. No one expected to run into members of the Carnegie family when attending a show at Carnegie Hall in New York City, or any Kennedys while flying out of New York's JFK airport. Apparently, this was just a special Jack Endicott Sutton twist.

Still, she should have put it together when she'd seen him, instead of being so dizzied by her overwhelming reaction to him. She should have done a lot of things, including never surrendering to that reaction, that deadly attraction, in the first place five years ago. *Should have* might as well be tattooed across her forehead, she thought then, glowering at herself in the cracked mirror as she climbed from the tub and wrapped a towel around herself. It was the story of her life.

She was pulling on a soft T-shirt over a pair of yoga pants when the peremptory knock sounded at the door. Larissa froze, her heart going wild. There was only one person it could be. Only one person she'd spoken more than a few words to since she'd arrived. Only one, and she knew better than to let him in. She'd be safer donning a red cape and wandering through the nearest forest, looking for wolves.

And yet she found herself crossing the small room as if compelled, as if he ordered her to do so simply by his presence on the other side of the door. Her bare feet, still warm from the bath, scuffed against the rough-hewn wood beams in the floor. Her breasts seemed to swell against her shirt, as a kind of glimmering wound low in her belly, and pulsed. She was aware of the cheerful comforter spread across the tidy double bed, the rain and wind buffeting the small round windows that lined the wall above it. She was aware of her own wet hair, her own damp skin. She was suddenly as hot as she'd been in the tub; hotter. As if that simple, demanding knock had set her ablaze.

He did not knock again. He did not have to. She could sense him there, on the other side of the wood. She could *see* him—that dark, stirring gaze. That absurdly distracting mouth. Those perfect, sculpted cheekbones and that strong nose, the unmistakable stamp of his ancestors and the easy, rangy athleticism that was uniquely his. The towering intellect behind it that had allowed him to transform so easily from black sheep reprobate to the chairman of his family's foundation—an evolution that had endeared him even more to his legion of admirers. He was beautiful, but he was no pretty boy. He never had been, not even when he'd played the part so easily, so well, for so long. It was yet one more reason he was the most dangerous man she'd ever met.

Five years ago, even in the damaged state she'd been in, she'd known that well enough to walk away from him. So why, now, with so much more of herself to lose, did she do precisely the opposite of what she knew she should?

She was a fool beyond the telling of it, in ways she could not even bear to examine, and even so, she swung open the door. She could not seem to stop herself. She could not seem to *want* to stop herself.

He loomed there in the doorway, his body too big in the narrow, shadowy hallway, dark and hungry-eyed. She could see the stark, mouthwatering outline of his lean arms as he braced them above the door, the carved beauty of his chest as he hung there as if on display, like some impossible piece of sculpture. And then she met his bittersweet brown gaze and lost her breath completely.

He is much too dangerous and you are far too weak, she railed at herself, but he was right there in front of her, making her heart do cartwheels against her ribs, and she had always been helpless where this man was concerned, no matter what she let on. No matter what stories she told herself. Always.

Jack stepped over the threshold, forcing Larissa either to back up or let him bump against her. She chose to move back, deeper into the room, and cursed herself when she saw the faint hint of a smile curve his devastating mouth. Jack, she knew, was a master of power games. He could hardly hold the position he held at the Endicott Foundation, or in their bright and complicated little society world, without that kind of mastery. She jerked her attention away from his distracting mouth.

"You overstated your ownership of this island somewhat," she said, deciding that offense was far preferable to defense, and pretending she didn't feel stripped bare despite the fact she was wearing clothes. She had to fight to keep her arms from crossing over her chest, a protective gesture he would read too easily and, she had no doubt, use against her.

It was something about the laser-hot gaze he let drift over her, the way the air around them seemed to tighten, making her feel almost light-headed. Almost dizzy. That, she told herself, was why she felt so off balance around this man. It was chemical. Nothing more. And she was done with chemicals, too.

"I never overstate," he replied, though his eyes were on her lips, touching them as if he was think-ing of kissing her, of claiming her, even then. As if he already had. Her thighs clenched hard against the sudden spike of heat through her core. He met her gaze slowly, insolently. "I don't have to."

"Your family owned the island once," she said crisply, rattling off the results of the search she'd cued up on her smartphone. "But your grandfa-ther gave most of it over to the Maine Coast Heri-tage Trust some thirty years ago, and some more to the State of Maine long before that. Now you simply sit in your grand old estate, the patriarch that never was, staring out over the land that could have been yours." She forced a light little laugh. "How sad."

"I'm flattered," he said, moving farther into the room. Larissa stood her ground, even though her legs felt wobbly, and the small room seemed to shrink in around him, trapping her. "Did you rush back to your room to research me, Larissa? Or did you already know everything you needed to know about me before you came to the island in the first place?"

"That's a loaded question, I think," she retorted, refusing to move even as he drifted closer, even as his shoulders seemed to block out the whole of the far wall. He was not *actually* growing larger before her very eyes, she told herself sharply. It was just that damned chemical reaction again, her body's helpless response to him, making her crazy. "I've known you since I was a child. There's very little I *don't* know about you, directly or indirectly." She waved a languid hand as if none of it interested her in the least. "Except for your inner thoughts, of course—assuming you have any of those." She smirked. "I've found that men of your great consequence and vast self-importance most often do not."

"I think you are confusing the two of us," Jack replied softly, his dark eyes glittering, as if he could not decide whether he found her amusing or irritating. "I am not the one rumored to be the most vapid creature in all of Manhattan, if not the entire country. Quite a feat, Larissa. How proud you must be."

She felt a stab of something like pain, like shame, shoot through her and shoved it aside. The tabloids said all that and worse, daily. They had done since she was a teenager, and *vapid* was practically a compliment in comparison to the things they called her. What should she care if he joined in the chorus? Why should it matter that he did so to her face, with every appearance of believing it? She told herself such things could hardly matter to her any longer. She should be entirely immune.

"Oh, come now," she said, clucking her tongue. She did not let her gaze drift to that intoxicating hollow between his pectoral muscles, lovingly outlined by his shirt. She did not let her eyes travel further south to investigate that washboard of an abdomen. "You remember—I've known you forever. I knew you back before you decided to reinvent yourself, back before you became the most boring man alive. I knew you when you were *fun*." She shrugged, knowing she looked careless and amused. Effortless. Blasé. It was her greatest talent. "Back when you were, if I recall it correctly, voted the most dissipated playboy in all of New York City every year for the better part of your twenties."

She'd run into him, fatefully, at the tail end of that period, she thought, willing those unhelpful and unnecessary memories away. Right when he'd been teetering on the edge of respectability in the wake of his beloved mother's death. For all she knew, their little weekend tryst had been the straw that broke him. Just one more sin to add to her roster, no doubt. She had given up counting them all.

"Is that why you hate me so much, with so little reason?" she asked then, spurred by some emotion she hardly understood, some small glimpse of something in his expression that she barely comprehended. "Because I knew you when? That hardly seems fair. So does most of Manhattan."

"I don't hate you, Larissa," he said, his voice a rough caress in the small room, abrading her skin, making her arch slightly against it, as if he'd really touched her. "I know you."

He reached over then, and tracked a leftover droplet from her bath down the side of her neck, across her collarbone, his finger scorching her. Terrifying her. Her gaze was trapped in his. Fire. Anger. And something else, something darker, that she was afraid to explore.

That, God help her, made her *want. Yearn.*

"What are you doing?" she asked, hating herself for the breathlessness in her voice, the weakness spreading through her. The helpless wanting that even so small a touch could evoke in her. He was an exercise in self-immolation. And he was entirely too addictive, a quick slide into nothing but madness. She'd escaped him once, but she had no reason to believe she would be so lucky again. In fact, she knew better.

But she didn't move. She didn't step away.

His lips twitched and a very male triumph lit his dark gaze. She hated that even more.

"It occurred to me that there is very little do here on Endicott Island," he said, his finger toying with the V-neck of her shirt, teasing her. Yet—still—there was a measuring coolness in his eyes. As if he was testing as much as teasing her. "And we wouldn't want you bored. I've seen what happens when you get bored." He let out a small laugh. "The whole world has, I imagine."

"I'm very easily bored, and just as easily photographed, it's true," she agreed, forcing the breathlessness back into remission. Covering the hurt she shouldn't allow herself to feel with a sniff. "I'm bored right now."

He only smiled.

"While you're here so unexpectedly," he said, his fingers drawing out an intoxicating rhythm inside of her, making it pulse deep into her core, "we might as well remind ourselves of the one thing we're really, really good at, don't you think?"

She had the urge to play dumb, to ask him

what he meant, but the glittering light in his gaze stopped her. She was afraid he would demonstrate what he meant, and how could she possibly survive that? He thought she was the same person she'd been eight months ago, the same person she'd been five years ago. Brittle, hard. Empty. Capable of withstanding anything without truly letting it touch her. *Numb.* He would treat her like the girl he'd known then, that ghost of herself, that walking shadow. And in so doing, he would ruin whoever she was now, softer and quieter and certainly no match for the likes of him.

She couldn't allow it. She wouldn't.

But she also couldn't let him see that she'd changed. It would end the same way, and she would lose so much more. He would assume it was a trick, a game. He would accuse her of ulterior motives. And Larissa couldn't defend herself, could she? She couldn't explain what had happened to her, much less who she'd become—she was still in the process of figuring that out.

And she was so deathly afraid of the answer.

"I thought you said one taste was more than enough," she tossed back at him lightly, surprised to find that the words still stung. She knew they shouldn't. What was one more low opinion? She smiled up at him, mysterious, unknowable. The Larissa Whitney promise. Her impenetrable armor. "But no need to worry. Most men, like you, can't even begin to handle me."

His smile bordered on feral. She felt it hard in her belly, like a kick, and then his eyes went dark.

She stopped breathing.

"Watch me," he said hoarsely.

And then his hands were on her shoulders, warm and sure. And she was lost.

He pulled her close, his lips twisting slightly into something too hard to be a smile, and then he took her mouth in a searing, impossible kiss.

CHAPTER THREE

IT WAS worse than she'd remembered, when she'd allowed herself to remember him at all. It was better.

So much better.

Hotter, sleeker, rolling through her like a tornado, tearing her apart, making her shake as the wild passion claimed her. Her hands found his narrow hips, the taut, smooth muscles of his back, and despite herself, she clung. His skin was so warm, so firm, blazing through the tight shirt he wore, making her long to reach beneath it.

She felt him everywhere.

He kissed her again and again, as if he was as swept away in this fire, this madness, as she was. As if he never meant to stop. Her toes curled against the floorboards. Her eyes fell shut, her back arched, bringing her closer to his drugging heat. She ached everywhere he touched her, and ached even more where he did not. She melted. She burned.

She was in so much trouble.

She was not drunk this time, feeling daring and careless and out of control after a long night at a chaotic party. She was not numbed and halfway to dead inside. There was nothing to dull the exquisite force of him or her own helpless, needy reaction, and however dangerous she had believed him to be before, she knew now she had greatly underestimated his power over her.

She was such a fool.

And still she kissed him back, angling her mouth for a better fit, moving closer in his arms, pressing up against the hard wall of his chest. She couldn't seem to help herself. It was as if he'd been created just for her, carefully constructed to make her lose her mind.

But she was not the same girl he'd once known, however peripherally—not the same person at all any longer, and it was that thought that finally penetrated the delirious fog in her brain. She knew what she was doing here, with him—what she was risking. But he was still playing old games, settling old scores. She knew it, no matter how good he tasted, how perfectly they fitted. She couldn't let that matter.

She couldn't lie to herself—hadn't she made herself that vow?—and pretend that letting this happen would do anything but destroy her.

For good this time. She could feel the truth of

that deep inside of her, like some kind of primal feminine knowledge she'd never accessed before.

She tore her mouth from his and backed up then, as she should have done from the start. *Better late than never,* she told herself. Another mantra that could apply to her whole life these days. It was cold comfort.

"Well," she said lightly, easily, pretending she couldn't feel him still, that her whole body did not ache, yearn, *need.* That her heart was not still thudding, hard and insistent, her blood racing wild and excited through her veins. "Apparently you handle things quite well. But I think I'll have to decline."

"Why?" The single word was almost a laugh, arrogant and sure, his gaze frankly incredulous as it seared into hers, invitation and temptation. And that impossible fire that always burned between them, that seductive blaze.

Why, indeed?

But she was not the old Larissa, the heedless Larissa who thought only of a moment's pleasure—the better to avoid thinking about anything else. She could not play games with this man and skip away unscathed. And she was very much afraid that she had already damaged herself beyond repair.

So she shrugged, pulling the familiar mantle of *Larissa Whitney, heartless, careless flirt* around her like the armor it was. Her favorite disguise. Because she did not dare let this man see anything more, anything deeper. She did not dare show him anything he could destroy.

"Because you want it too much," she said airily, turning away from him and drifting toward the fireplace as if she could dismiss him that easily. She closed her eyes for a tight, brief moment—for strength—and then glanced over her shoulder at him, and smiled. Saucily. As if she wanted nothing more than to tease him. "Where's the fun in that?"

He shouldn't have done that. He shouldn't have touched her, much less kissed her. Jack could see the passion in her green eyes, making them luminous. He wanted to make them glaze over with heat. Her mouth was still swollen slightly from his, and he wanted to taste her again. She was narcotic. And still she played her damned games. Lies within lies, like the Russian dolls his mother had collected.

Why was he surprised? That was the real question, and one Jack knew he should investigate. But instead, he watched her.

"I didn't realize I scared you so much," he drawled, injecting a note of mockery into his tone, knowing it would get her back up, refusing to question why he wanted that reaction. Any reaction. "I thought nothing could."

"Bats," she said immediately, that charming lilt to her voice, the one that made her so impossible to dismiss. The one that made her seem like some latter-day Holly Golightly. "And scorpions." She gave a mock shudder. "But you? I'm afraid not, Jack. I know that must come as a grave disappointment."

"I know why you're here." It grated out of him, more angrily than it should have. "You can stop all your playacting and simply admit it."

She glanced back at him again, still standing before the fire, damp and delectable from a bath he could imagine in all-too-graphic detail, her short dark hair slightly mussed and entirely too alluring. He could not seem to reconcile himself to the dissonance—to the fragility of her delicate bones, her waiflike figure, juxtaposed with that cold, heartless core of emptiness he knew was the hidden truth of her, holding her up like a spine. She was indestructible, for all she looked like the next gust of bitter wind against the rattling windows might blow her over.

And those eyes of hers should have been hard as stones, but reminded him instead of the sea. His beloved, unknowable Atlantic, forever complicated by the storms, the island's rocky shoreline, the towering wall of pines. Shadows chased through her mysterious gaze, then disappeared, leaving him to wonder if he'd imagined them.

"Why don't you tell me why I'm here?" she suggested, her voice low. She turned back to the fire, dismissal and disinterest stamped along every inch of her aristocratic back, the incline of her elegant neck. "Or we can just pretend that you already did. Don't worry, I'll be sure to add in the necessary insults in my memory of the conversation that never was. It will be just like the real thing."

There was a certain dryness to her tone, a certain dark humor, that he couldn't quite take in. It spoke to a kind of self-awareness he'd never believed she could be capable of achieving. He wished he could see her expression. If she had been another woman, he might even have entertained the possibility that he'd hurt her feelings. But this was Larissa. She didn't have any. Not the way other people did. Not unless she could use them as leverage.

He let his gaze travel over her celebrated body, admiring her despite himself. How could he not? She was one of the great beauties of the age, or so the media claimed with predictable regularity. And he had tested the theory with his own hands. He knew all of those fine, patrician lines. The curve of her spine, the swell of her hips, the delectable round thrust of her bottom. He knew that soft place just below her hairline at the nape of her neck. He knew what would happen if he pressed his mouth to it, the little gasp she would make, the way her whole body would arch and then shudder.

He found the simple black pants she wore, the small, snug T-shirt, her feet bare against the floorboards, far more erotic and captivating than any of the many elaborate costumes he'd seen her in before. Almost as if she was not as out of place here as he believed her to be. But he was not likely to share that kind of thought, not with a woman like Larissa, and not when it was no doubt proof of his own abiding insanity. She would only use it against him somehow. Everything was a weapon. Everything and everyone had a use. He knew that better than anyone.

She was some kind of witch, though he knew others preferred a different word to describe her, and he had spent years trying to figure out why he'd fallen so hard beneath her spell. Why she had haunted him when so many other women had failed to make any impression at all. He had a thousand different theories, but he still didn't have an answer. And it hardly mattered any longer.

"I feel suitably chastised," she said, making him aware of his own brooding silence. She turned around then, her skin flushed from the fire, her eyes darker than they should have been. But her smile was the same as it ever was. That impertinent curve of her lips—as alluring as it was concealing. He should not have this insane urge to try to figure her out. He should not find her so damned fascinating, despite his best intentions.

"See?" Again, that saucy little quirk of her lips. "No need to have the conversation at all. Feel free to let yourself out."

"The Whitney Media Board of Directors meets next month," Jack said before he knew he meant to speak. He watched her wince slightly, then check it, and thought he'd landed a blow. He had the impression that she forced herself to resume her usual air of disinterested bonelessness—and felt something move in him in response. He called it cynicism. Weariness. After all, he'd just exposed her little game, hadn't he?

"You really have become the most tedious man," she said softly, a light in those captivating eyes he couldn't read. "I can't think of anything I would rather discuss less while in the middle of a storm on a lonely little island than Whitney Media."

"I've heard rumors," he said. He tracked her, his eyes narrowing, as she drifted over to the armchair near the fire and folded herself into it, drawing her knees up beneath her. "Everyone has."

"Manhattan runs on rumors, I find," she said in the same easy tone that he found disturbed him in ways he did not care to examine. "The city that never sleeps because it is far too busy whispering salacious tales into every willing ear, stirring up as much dirt as possible before dawn." She shrugged as if it was no matter to her, the prurient interest of others. "The veracity of said dirt is never important, of course."

"You need to appear at that meeting, don't you?" he countered, because he didn't need to listen to any stories about her—he'd lived them. "You were very smart to stay out of the papers these past months. But now you need to prove to your father and his disapproving cronies that you've become truly respectable, or they'll declare you unfit and appoint a proxy to vote your shares of the company."

He wasn't saying anything any businessman wouldn't know, simply from reading opinion pieces in the *Wall Street Journal*. And yet her emerald gaze seemed to simmer with something that might have been anger, had she been someone else. But then she smiled that Mona Lisa smile at him.

"You say that as if I have been in a pitched battle for control of the company since my eighteenth birthday, like some desperate heroine on a daytime soap opera," she murmured. One delicate hand went to her neck, as if testing the shape of her collarbone beneath her fingers. In another woman, he would call it a nervous tic, a telling gesture. But this was Larissa. She had no tells, only traps. She met his gaze without apparent distress. "I hate to disabuse you of your melodramatic notions, but I've had a proxy vote for me for as long as I can remember." She made a face. "I can't really think of anything that would bore me more deeply than a board meeting. Particularly if that board had anything to do with a company I was tired of hearing about before I reached kindergarten." Her perfectly arched brows rose. Her stormy gaze was cool. Deceptively so, he thought. "As you already know, I really don't like to be bored."

"Your father and your former fiancé handled your shares," Jack said ruthlessly, ignoring her performance. Because what else could it be? What else could bring her here but her own self-interest? He didn't know why she thought she could hide it—or why she bothered to try. "But your fiancé, who was always your champion, has disappeared and everyone knows you are no favorite of your father's. This meeting may be your only chance to wrest control of your own inheritance for the foreseeable future."

That was the squalid little truth, he thought, watching her face now that he'd slapped that down on the table, out in the open, between them. He thought a faint flush rose high on her cheekbones, but it could as easily have been the heat of the crackling fire.

He wanted her to admit it. To admit that this was why she'd turned up here, like his own personal ghost. That he was only the means to an end. He knew exactly what securing him—marrying him, even—would do for Larissa, what it would mean for her reputation and prospects. He should be more sympathetic to her plight. Weren't his grandfather's latest decrees about Jack's duty to marry well, and soon, much the same kind of pressure? Wasn't he taking this time on the island to come to terms with that inevitability? He really ought to relate.

But Larissa sighed, musical and put-upon all at once, and any sympathy he might have had vanished. They were nothing alike. Jack spent every moment of his day doing his duty, making himself the worthy successor to his family's legacy. Larissa only wanted unrestricted access to her family's money, the better to spend her life shopping it all away. He felt his jaw tense.

"I have other sources of income," she said, waving a hand as if such sources grew thick in the trees. But then, in their world of endless privilege, stretching back across centuries, they often did. "It was Theo who was so obsessed with Whitney Media. He and my father and their high-stakes corporate games. I begin to nod off to sleep whenever the topic comes up. I'm getting remarkably drowsy now."

Jack laughed then, despite himself, and moved across the room in a few sure steps. He leaned down toward her, bracing himself on the arms of the chair, bringing his face far too close to hers as he trapped her in her seat.

"Let me tell you what I think," he said, satisfaction surging through him at the faint alarm that flashed across her face. At least it was an honest reaction. *Any* reaction.

"If you feel you must," she drawled, but he could see the pulse beat against the tender flesh of her neck, and he knew she was not nearly as unmoved as she pretended. He leaned closer.

"I think that you came to this island in the worst of the fall storms to drag me into this little battle you pretend you don't care about." He could smell her scent again, and it made his body harden, though he still held himself just slightly apart from her. There were many forms of revenge, after all, and not all of them required that he betray himself. "As you keep pointing out, I have become so boring, haven't I? Positively respectable. Not one of your usual doomed bad-boy projects or untrustworthy celebrity lovers. I'd be the perfect ally, wouldn't I, Larissa? I'd make you look reborn. Your father would eat right out of your hand if you brought him me on a silver platter, wouldn't he?"

It was a fantastic plan, Larissa thought, her eyes searching his dark, commanding gaze. Brilliant, even. Nothing thrilled her father more than pedigrees that matched and/or exceeded his own. Bradford Whitney cared about nothing at all save the Whitney legacy, by which he meant his own continued wealth and consequence and all that entailed. Larissa had long been a grave disappointment to him in this area.

When she had brought Theo Markou Garcia home as her boyfriend, and had eventually made him her fiancé, she had mostly been interested in the fact that he came from absolutely nothing—a sin she'd been certain Bradford could never overlook. But she had underestimated Theo. He had taken over the company, becoming the son Bradford had never had in the process. That he had finally left her was, Larissa knew, something Bradford would never find it in him to forgive her. Much less the fact that Theo's near-miraculous ability as CEO to make Whitney Media rake in profits had disappeared with him.

But Jack Endicott Sutton would be exactly the right kind of salve for Bradford's bruised ego and slightly depressed portfolio. Any suggestion that Larissa, the great disappointment and stain upon the Whitney name, could link herself to a man like Jack? The single heir to two separate great American families, from Mayflower Boston and Upper Ten Thousand New York both—and the vast fortunes that came with each? A man who had transformed himself from notorious if beloved rake to dependable, hardworking, worthy successor to all his family's innumerable riches? Bradford would be beside himself.

Larissa imagined that somewhere in the depths of the iconic Whitney mansion that sprawled over a whole city block on Fifth Avenue in Manhattan, her father was suddenly filled with an unimaginable if unclear joy, simply because the very *idea* of linking the Gilded Age splendor of the Whitney name to the august Bostonian Endicotts and the clever Sutton robber-barons-turned-bankers had occurred to someone, somewhere. It would be like his personal Christmas.

But, of course, she'd had no such plan. She'd been running away from all of that noise and obligation since the day she'd woken up from her coma, more or less, and she'd had no plans to return to New York City at all—much less to Whitney Media, and she'd certainly had no plans to involve herself in some doomed scheme toward respectability with Jack Sutton.

Jack was the very last man she would ever have sought out. Ever. She couldn't trust herself anywhere near him, as tonight had already proven beyond any shadow of a doubt. But, of course, in order to explain to him why that was so, she would be forced to admit the kind of power he had always had over her. She couldn't do it. There was too much to lose—and anyway, she was used to his low opinion of her. It was nothing new. She told herself it hardly even hurt.

"So quiet," he murmured, taunting her, his voice snapping her back into the tense, dangerous present. Where his mouth was much too close to hers, his eyes were much too knowing, and the banked fire he lit in her was stoked to a worrying blaze already. "Did you really think that you could fool me? Did you imagine that your presence here would be casual in some way? This island is as inhospitable as they come. There can be no reason at all for you to be here at this time of year. None. Save one."

"You are so conceited," she managed to say, fighting her voice's urge toward a much-too-telling tremor.

"You're a terrible actress," he replied, far too easily.

He squatted down in front of her chair, still caging her between his strong arms, but now his muscled thighs spread open before her and his face, his mouth, were much too close to hers. She dared not move. He was so big, so male, and as dangerous as he was compelling. She wanted to leap out of this chair and run, screaming, from the room—the inn—the island. But more than that, she wanted to lean forward and touch him. Both propositions were terrifying.

"Why don't you just admit what you came for?" His voice was mocking. Knowing. Insinuating.

Larissa sucked in a deep breath. And then, because she knew that he would never believe her, that he saw only what he wanted to see—only what she'd worked so hard to show to the world for so long, and never anything else, never anything beneath that mask—she told him the truth.

"I had no idea you'd be here," she said quietly. Matter-of-factly. Because she found she needed to say it, and it was safe here, now, where she would never be believed. Perhaps not even heard. His expression was already shifting to one of total disbelief. "It never occurred to me that there would be an Endicott in residence on Endicott Island. Why would it, at this time of year? I just put my car on the ferry headed for the most remote place I could find, and here I am. There's no plot. No grand scheme to prove something to my father. I've thought as little about him—and Whitney Media—as possible."

His mouth flattened, as if she'd disappointed him—again. She was entirely too familiar with that particular expression. And she told herself she was an idiot if she expected anything different, even from him. Even for a second.

"Of course not," he said sardonically. "Because you've suddenly been seized with your typical wanderlust, except for some reason you chose this island instead of, say, Rio. The Amalfi coast. Anywhere in the South Pacific."

That he didn't believe her was practically written across him, tattooed onto his smooth warm skin. Flashing before her like all the bright lights of New York City. And, therefore, it was safe for her to tell him truths she would never have dared mention if she'd had the slightest worry he might believe them.

This is who you are, a small voice pointed out inside of her, condemning her. *This twisted thing, good for nothing but lies and truths hidden away like ciphers.*

"Maybe I'm trying to reinvent myself," she said, making sure she smirked as she said it, making sure he couldn't give her words any weight, any resonance. "Maybe this is simply part of a period of reinterpretation." She shrugged her shoulders. "A deserted island in the late fall rains. What better place for rediscovery?"

He shook his head, letting his hands move from the arms of the chair. He touched her, tracing a pattern along her curled-up legs from knees to ankles, making that fire rage and burn anew. Then, unexpectedly, he took her hands between his. Her heart jolted in her chest. So hard she stopped breathing.

"You're so pretty when you lie," he said, almost tenderly, which made the words feel that much more like knives. Sharp and brutal. "You make it into a kind of art. You should be proud of it, I think."

She didn't know why she should feel so heartbroken, so sick, as if he'd ripped her into tiny pieces by acting as she'd known he would—as she'd wanted him to act. What did she expect? That somehow, Jack Endicott Sutton would see through all her layers of defense and obfuscation to what lay beneath? She didn't want that. She'd never wanted that. So why did it hurt so much that he didn't do it anyway?

But she knew why. She'd always known. There was something between them—something that sang in her whenever he touched her, something in the way he looked at her, that made her imagine things could be different. That *she* could be different. She hadn't been able to cope with the idea of that five years ago. And whatever he'd seen in her then, she'd ruined it. She knew she had, because that was what she did. That was who she was. She ruined whatever she touched.

Why should Jack be any different?

"I see," she said. She looked down at their hands, linked now, the heat of that connection moving through her in ways she should not allow. But she didn't move. She angled a look at him. "You are permitted to have a disreputable past, and then change when it suits you. But not me. Is that because you're a man?"

"It's because you're Larissa Whitney," he replied, and there was laughter in his gaze then. She wished it warmed her instead of chilling her to the bone. She wished she could drop this act, and make him really, truly believe her. She thought she could, if she dared enough. If she was brave enough.

But she had never been anything but weak. She doubted she ever would be. She took the easy road, because at least that way she could keep part of herself hidden. Safe. She had always tried too hard to keep something, somewhere, some kind of safe. Surely that counted for something.

And even if it didn't, it was all she had.

"Fine, then," she said, smiling back at him, even letting out her own little laugh in reply. Letting herself seem complicit—in on the joke. The very idea of her changing was *hilarious,* wasn't it? Impossible! She should know. She was the one trying to do it.

"Come have dinner with me." Jack's voice was rich and dark, and made her yearn for things she couldn't have, things she knew he'd never offer. Made her heart beat too fast, her blood pump too quickly through her limbs. He was seduction incarnate, and the worst part, she knew, was that he didn't really want her. Not *her.* He wanted the projection. The act. He wanted who he thought she was. And still, even knowing that, she wanted him like this. Like she might die if she didn't taste him again.

"Said the spider to the fly," she replied, smiling over the crack in her voice, pretending she was trying to sound husky, alluring.

"I think we both know that the only one here weaving any webs is you," Jack said. But he didn't seem to care about that. There was a cool, assessing glint in his dark gaze, as if he was reading her too closely. He stood up then, pulling her to her feet in an easy, offhand demonstration of his effortless strength, his matter-of-fact physical prowess. It made her feel fluttery. "And who knows? Maybe you can convince me to be a part of your little plot after all. Why not try?"

He was so arrogant. So sure that he saw right through her, that he knew everything. All her games. All her plans. The whole of her shallow little self. She didn't know if she wanted to punch him—or burst into tears. She wisely decided to do neither. She doubted he would react well to either extreme. And she doubted she would recover.

"Why should I?" she asked lightly, though it cost her to keep up the act. "You appear to already have your mind made up."

"Convince me," he said, in that low, stirring voice. His dark eyes were molten hot, so hungry and yet so shrewd, and they made her ache. They made her feel vulnerable, foolish. *Lost.* And then he smiled, and made everything that much worse. "I dare you."

CHAPTER FOUR

THE Endicott house dominated the southern half of the small island, announcing its grandeur and former ownership of all it surveyed in stark, unmistakable terms. The private lane wound down along the rugged, rain-lashed coast, no doubt affording spellbinding views toward the mainland on clear summer days, and then etched a path through the thick and silent woods. Pine trees stretched like tall, silent sentries on all sides, blocking out the dark, starless sky far above. Only when the narrow road finally climbed the last, far hill did the house reveal itself in all its glory, straddling the summit as it squared off, genteel and well-mannered, against the sea beyond.

Larissa was no stranger to beautiful, even iconic houses. She had lived in them all of her life. And yet she still felt her heart beat a little bit faster as she took that final turn in the battered, rocky dirt road. She let the car slow, and looked up at what Jack, with his typical upper-class New England understatement, had referred to as the Endicott "summer cottage." Like most seasonal dwellings of the same type, all belonging to members of the same blue-blooded social strata as Jack, the house had a name. This one was called Scatteree Pines. It was an affectation of the very wealthy, Larissa well knew, with their multiple houses in various destinations, to distinguish them by the names bestowed upon the different polished plaques that hung near each front door.

This was her world, too, Larissa reminded herself sharply. So why did she feel so much like an alien, set down into it but never quite of it? That was the million-dollar question, wasn't it?

The rain pounded down on the roof of the car, washing over the front window despite the energetic efforts of the windshield wipers, drumming into her head, her battered heart, her traitorous limbs. She didn't know which storm was more dangerous—the one with all the rain and the wind outside the confines of the car, or the far more damaging one inside her.

But she couldn't let herself think about that. She glared through the window, staring at the blurry, watery house that stood so proud and pretty before her, plump and confident in the dark, wet night.

She didn't know why she'd let the car drift to a stop like this, gawking up at the place as if she'd never seen a grand old house before. As if she was

some poor country mouse on her first trip somewhere special. As if she hadn't, in fact, grown up
in one of the most coveted remaining mansions in
New York City, the toast of what was left of the
Gilded Age Manhattan lifestyle. Perhaps it was
because this particular house was so…private.

Scatteree Pines sat up on the highest part of the
hill, its unobstructed view of the whole of the Atlantic Ocean that spread out from the rocks below,
its elegant back to the tiny village as if it held itself quietly apart, aloof. The house was a gabled,
grand old affair that nodded toward the Victorian
style, with a pitched central roof and two sprawling wings that spread away from the arresting
front entrance. But it was located down a long and
winding private drive in the farthest corner of one
of the most remote islands in North America. It
was not, like the Whitney summer "cottage" in
self-consciously posh Newport, Rhode Island, located squarely on the tourist-ridden and world-fa-
mous Cliff Walk, the better to impress the passing
unwashed masses with the storied Whitney legacy
and its fifty-plus rooms of gilt-edged opulence.

But that shouldn't matter, Larissa told herself
sharply. Scatteree Pines was no more a quiet little
"cottage" than Jack himself was the everyday sort
of man he'd been masquerading as today. Maybe
she'd needed this reminder. Maybe his battered old
jeans and casual T-shirt had confused her, making

her forget that whatever else Jack was, whatever he seemed to do to her with his slightest glance, he was one of the wealthiest men in the world. He came from a very long line of equally wealthy men, dating back to the original Colonies and before that, to a very elite selection of powerful and well-connected men in England. He was the heir to centuries of power, and he wore it with the carelessness of perfect comfort, evident in every cell and sinew of his well-toned body. She needed to remember that he knew exactly how to wield that power, and would do so—did do so—with absolutely no compunction.

Just like her own father. Just like all the sparkling and profoundly vicious people she knew— and had run from eight months ago. And yet here she was, trotting out in the pouring rain to have dinner at his command, even when she suspected *dinner* was a euphemism. She was sitting outside his door like an overwrought teenager, having driven herself right over, the very picture of obedience—and there was no gun to her head. No force, no compulsion. He'd only dared her.

And she, ever the moth to the most convenient and most disastrous flame, wherever it might burn and the more destructive the better, had come running. How could she explain that away?

He'd kissed her again before he'd left—a hard, branding press of his clever mouth to hers while his large hand had covered the nape of her neck. Keeping her still, and easy to plunder. Claiming her, she'd thought with some mix of panic and dizzy desire—marking his territory. And then he'd stalked off into the wet night with a muttered curse as if he hadn't meant to do that, leaving her to shake and shudder in his wake.

Damn him.

The trouble with islands was that there was no running away, she'd thought then, and thought again now as she sat, paralyzed, in the front seat of a rented Dodge Calibre that smelled of old pine deodorizer and the stale air of the incompetent defroster. And Larissa had absolutely no doubt that should she fail to appear at Jack's table tonight as he wished, as he had commanded, he would come find her. She'd decided it would be better to walk knowingly into his lair than let him trap her once again in hers.

But who was she kidding? What kind of story was she trying to sell herself? She let out a slight, bitter laugh.

She had promised not to lie to herself, no matter what. No matter the provocation. No matter that it would be so much easier than the inevitably painful truth. A great wave of shame, her now-familiar companion, crashed through her then, making her breath catch in her throat as her stomach knotted hard, and heat speared the back of her eyes. She was so damnably weak. Didn't she prove it to herself again and again and again?

She had been on the run for months—hiding from her past, hiding from herself. From her old ways and her old friends, her dirty, shameful history. And she'd been so proud of herself—or she'd been getting there. *Look at me, nowhere near Manhattan, barely recognizable any longer,* she'd thought to herself, running her hands through the short black hair that still surprised her—that she sometimes dreamed was still long, blond and lustrous. *Look at my self-imposed exile, my willingness to disguise myself. I can be new, different. I can change.*

She'd been the closest she'd ever come to *real.* That was what she'd been thinking as she'd stared out at the Maine storm, the dangerous, exhilaratingly powerful sea. She'd felt battered and bruised, and undoubtedly shaky—but for the first time, she'd also felt truly *alive.*

And then Jack Sutton had sauntered into that bar, temptation in perfect male form, the ultimate symbol of her old life and her dissolute past—and eight months of committed soul-searching disappeared. Ash and smoke, as if they had never happened. As if she'd learned nothing.

How could she have so little self-control, even now? Despair and something else, something uglier, flooded through her. How could she ignore everything she knew, everything she was only beginning to admit she needed, for a man who had never done anything but make her act like the worst version of herself?

How could she possibly justify her presence here tonight? How was it anything but the worst kind of backsliding into the very pit she'd been so determined to climb her way out of? Her very first test, and she'd already failed it with flying colors.

This is who you are, that little voice, her father's voice, whispered deep inside of her—so harsh and, she feared, so true. *This is what you do. Fail. Disappoint. And then fail again.*

She pressed her fingers to her mouth, as if pushing back the small sob that escaped her lips. She didn't have to do this. She threw the car into reverse—but even as she did it, before she could even lift her foot from the brake pedal, the grand doors of Scatteree Pines swung open, spilling light out across the drive. Larissa froze.

Jack stood there, tall and imposing in the great entryway, his dark eyes immediately slamming into hers through the windshield, across the storm. Connecting hard with that shaky part of her where her spine should have been. Making her shiver with a dizzying sense of helplessness. With the inevitability of this. With her own terrible need that she hardly understood.

She couldn't seem to breathe. Her heart was

like a cannonball, ricocheting against her ribs. She knew she needed to leave. She knew it. Before she let the tears fall, let the wildness within her out of its cage. Before she betrayed herself even further than she already had.

But she parked the car instead. She turned the key in the ignition, and the engine clicked off.

She took one breath, and then another, and still Jack watched her. As if he had every confidence in the world that she would do exactly what he wanted her do. As if it were a foregone conclusion.

And she hated herself, because she did it.

She climbed out of the car slowly, and took a deep breath, pulling the clean, damp air deep into her lungs. She let her legs ease into holding her there, and made sure they'd support her. The rain had let up for the moment, though the wind was still fierce, raging all around—smelling of the sea and the cold, crisp inevitability of the coming winter. She could smell the tang of wood smoke and wet pine, the rich earth of the forest and the wild, coarse salt of the ocean. The night was dark and dense, like a velvet fist, though the great house before her blazed with light. She preferred the darkness, she thought, helplessly. She was so very tired of finding ways to disappear in the glare of all those spotlights.

Jack stood there, silently watching her, compelling her, and she couldn't tell if he was dark or light, or what he would do to her. What she would do. What she had already done by coming here, by climbing out of the car, by putting all of this into motion. Something in her felt drawn to him, called to him, on some deep, primitive level that hummed in her bones—but she knew better than to trust the things she wanted. They had only ever hurt her.

She told herself it was the deep, northern chill, the wet and windy fall storm, that made her tremble, made her feel so alive, so exhilarated. So scared. So unsure of everything, even the familiar tools she'd always used to hide so easily in plain sight, that she found so hard to summon now, when she needed them the most. *It's only the cold,* she thought.

But then Jack smiled at her, that peremptory, knowing curve of his beautiful mouth, and she knew better.

He wanted flippancy and fakeness, his preferred version of That Shallow Larissa Whitney, and so that was what she gave him, however much it cost her. She told herself she would deal with it later. She pulled in a deep breath and then breezed up the steps toward him, keeping her face as bland as it could be, pulling that persona around her like a familiar old cloak.

"No staff?" she asked mildly, sweeping past

him as if she was dripping in couture and trailed by a red carpet entourage instead of garbed in a pair of worn jeans and a turtleneck sweater, the better to wrap her traitorous body away from his beguiling, incendiary touch. Her boots came up to her knees and she was not in the least afraid to kick him with them, she told herself. In fact, she wanted to kick him. "I'm shocked to the core. I thought scions of such great families preferred to be waited upon, lest they forget their own greatness for even a moment."

"You would know more about that than I would," Jack said dryly. But his gaze locked to hers, and it made the world seem to tilt. Larissa looked away, shaken. It had never been so difficult to keep up her act before. Not even with him.

He had exchanged the T-shirt for a sweater in a rich burgundy cashmere that her fingers itched to touch, though his jeans remained the same, slung low on his narrow hips and clinging to his hard thighs like a pliant lover. Yet somehow, surrounded by this house, this unmistakable marker of who he really was, there was no possibility of pretending there was anything *everyday* about him. Larissa swallowed, and wordlessly handed him her heavy black peacoat and charcoal-gray scarf when he gestured for them, draping them over his arm as if he was a butler. Some part of her preferred the fantasy version of this man that she'd seen earlier in battered old jeans and work boots, as if he was just another local fisherman. As if that—or anything—could make him more palatable.

"I watched you sit out there in your car," he said, some kind of mockery in his voice, and something else, something darker, making his eyes gleam. "You looked…" He didn't finish the sentence. Larissa forced herself to smile, to be mysterious and unknowable. Empty, as he would expect. "Did you change your mind?"

"About what?" she asked idly. "Dinner?"

"That, too," he said. He disposed of her coat and then indicated that she should follow him, leading the way down a hallway only intermittently lit. Larissa concentrated on the house itself—far better, far safer that than the man who moved with such easy self-assurance in front of her, who strode ahead without glancing around, arrogantly expecting her to follow.

Which, of course, she did. Though she could not bring herself to focus on that grave personal failing—not just then. She looked at the house instead.

It was the particular conceit of a certain kind of New Englander, she knew, to treat their own vast wealth like some kind of embarrassing, potentially contagious disease. They kept their houses cold, the rugs threadbare. They drove depressingly practical cars into states of disrepair, found the slightest displays of wealth repulsive in the extreme, and went out of their way to avoid drawing attention to themselves in any capacity. The Puritan work ethic still ran like steel in their blue-blooded veins. Unlike many of Larissa's socialite peers, their philanthropic gestures were never empty. The Endicott family—particularly Jack's forbidding and formidable grandfather, she knew, as everyone knew—was precisely this sort of anti-aristocrat.

But despite all that, there was nothing at all shabby about the Endicott house. It was simply, quietly comfortable, on every level. The wealth of the Endicott family was evident everywhere, yet never overt. It was in the way the furniture was so well-maintained, despite the salt in the air and the fact that a summer house could not possibly see as much use as a primary residence. It was clear in the well-appointed ease of the sitting room Jack led her into, the quiet excellence that seemed to perfume the air.

It was as if people really lived here, she thought, maybe even a real family—and then she told herself she was being fanciful. A house was a house, and Jack was no different from anyone else in their empty little plastic-fishbowl world. There was no reason she ought to feel flushed with some kind of deep, pointless yearning for things that could not exist. Not for people like them.

She told herself it was only the fire, cheerful and bright, that warmed the room and took the edge off the night's chill. She felt unsteady—awkward—so she moved to the sofa and lowered herself onto it, assuming as languid a pose as she could without sliding off. Yet another one of her many skills. She should thank him for allowing her to showcase them all.

"Drink?" Jack was already moving toward the bar in the corner.

"By all means, anesthetize yourself," she said coolly. "I prefer a clear head while making huge mistakes."

Jack laughed, and ice cubes rattled against crystal. "Since when?"

She could only take that hit, which she'd walked right in to, and pretend it didn't sting.

"It's a recent affectation," she replied after a moment. "Didn't you rush to remind me that I just spent time in rehab?"

He threw her a dark, shrewd look. "Are you suggesting you took any of that seriously?" he asked, his voice too even. "You?"

Because that would be impossible, she thought bitterly. Larissa Whitney could never change. She would never want it, she could never do it even if she did want it, and—more to the point—no one would let her try. Why did she keep telling herself otherwise?

"I don't see why you'd bother," he continued far too easily, though when he turned, a tumbler of amber liquid in his hand, there was that dangerous light in his cool brown eyes.

"Maybe I'm following in your footsteps," she said, forcing herself not to look away. Forcing herself to raise her brows in challenge. "Maybe I'm refashioning myself, rehabilitating my tarnished image and starting all over. Brand-new. Just like you."

"I don't see why," he said, with an insulting flash of irritation in his gaze, as if he could not possibly imagine that anything she'd just said could have the slightest shred of truth in it. She was too far gone. Too lost.

She thought the same thing often enough, but Larissa found that when *he* concurred, she didn't like it. Not at all. It made something itchy and hard move through her, kicking the despair out of the way.

"Yes, well," she murmured, hating him—for a searing moment, even more than she hated herself. "There's a great deal you don't see, isn't there?"

He looked at her for a long moment. The tension between them pulled tight, crushing the air out of the room, out of her lungs. He didn't cross to her—but then, he didn't have to. He only kept that cool, too-astute gaze on her, and Larissa had to fight to keep all her rolling, storming emotions inside, locked away.

"I think I see all too clearly," he said. "You need a new, appropriate fiancé and you think you can manipulate me into doing your bidding. Why not? You're good at it, and we both know you've done it before."

There was no hint of heat now. There was only that cool assessment, that shattering calm. This, Larissa realized in a kind of panic, was the man he had become in the past five years. Perhaps the man he had always been. And he was not in the least bit blind.

"Did I manipulate you that weekend?" she managed to ask. She thrust aside any notion of Jack Sutton as her fiancé. It was too…much. She made herself smile, as if she felt cocky and amused. "I only remember leaving."

Something moved across his face then, but still, he only gazed at her for another long breath. She felt that shaking deep inside her, as if her very foundations stuttered when he was near.

"I will never do anything that might shake my grandfather's faith in me," he said and then smirked. "Tenuous as that faith may be, given the way I used to behave. It took me far too long to be the man I should have been, and I won't give him reason to doubt it. Do you understand me?"

She thought she understood him all too well. It made her feel sick. Despair and shame and a hard kick of temper collided inside her, knotting her stomach.

"Like, for example, if you were seen with the likes of me," she forced herself to say, amazed at how clear her voice was, at how calm she managed to sound. "That would soil you beyond redemption, surely."

He only watched her for a moment, as if he was waiting for a certain reaction. A temper tantrum? Something violent and shocking? Or perhaps he thought she might simply roll her eyes and shrug it off? Make some light little remark—make it flirtatious and somehow safe? Or perhaps all of the above?

"I'm sorry if that hurts your feelings," he said, in the way men did when they were not, in fact, the least bit apologetic. When they were only sorry that you hadn't genuflected in gratitude as they eviscerated you. "But it's the simple truth. You won't get what you want from me, Larissa. Not tonight, not ever. No matter what happens."

"What is it you think I want?" she asked, her voice a bare thread of sound. "And what do you think I'm willing to do to get it?"

And Jack only smiled, those dark eyes burning into her, the heat between them unmistakable. He stood there, so impossibly beautiful and so cruel, so confident that he could insult her like this, that she thought so little of herself that she would take it. That she would even use her body to try to sway him to her side—because he believed this was all some grand scheme of hers. That she was as obsessed with fortunes and spread sheets and inheritances as her family was—as he was.

That she would prostitute herself for it.

Another flash of temper ignited in her, setting off a chain—a wildfire. She had to take a breath to keep from letting it out in a scream of fury. At him, for believing such a thing. At herself, for having lived the kind of life that allowed for that impression.

She had never really gotten mad before, not really. She had always made certain to be too numb for that kind of thing. She'd always pushed unpleasant emotions off into other things—hidden them, or translated them into some other behavior, or acted them out in some other, inappropriate way.

But she wasn't that person anymore, no matter what Jack Sutton seemed to think. She wasn't. She wouldn't be.

There was something freeing, she thought in some detached part of her brain, that she could be *this* angry at *this* man right here, right now, in *this* moment. Surely that was progress, however scraped raw she felt.

But she knew, on some deep level, that simply screaming at him was not the answer. He would only see it as some kind of confirmation. So she forced herself to take a breath, and then she bared her teeth at him, not her pretty little public smile at all.

"I don't see the point of this conversation," she said. "If you're not going to play, why get in the game at all?"

"I want to see how far you'll go," he said at once—too quickly, she thought. His dark eyes were condemning now. His mouth twisted. "I want to see just how little shame you really have, Larissa."

God, how she hated him. What a hypocrite he was. As if his own past didn't look remarkably like her own! But if he wanted to play a game of chicken, she could do that, too. Because she knew that he was no more in control of the electricity sizzling between them than she was. She remembered that, if nothing else. And clearly he remembered it, too, or why else would he have brought her here to punish her?

He wasn't the only one who could call a bluff.

She stood then, slowly. Sinuously. Making sure his eyes tracked her every move—and smiling when they did.

"I'm shameless," she told him huskily, meeting his gaze. "But you know that already."

She hooked her fingers beneath the soft wool of her sweater, and then pulled it up and over her head.

She heard a quiet curse. And then the sweater was off. She tossed it to the side and then she stood naked to the waist before him, without so much as a bra between them. She'd never needed one, and so her breasts jutted out, proud and full as the cooler air caressed them, and she felt more powerful in that moment than she had in years. Like some kind of avenging goddess, the kind men like Jack Sutton should know better than to toy with.

"Put on your clothes," he rasped at her, a harsh command.

But she could see the bright, hard desire that glittered fierce and wild in his dark eyes. She could see the way his body tightened, the long, corded muscles in his neck and the long lines of his powerful body pulling taut. The way he clenched his hands. He tossed back the rest of his drink with a quick jerk and then slapped the tumbler down on the nearest table—but he didn't move away from her.

"Poor Jack," she taunted him, glorying in his weakness, thrilled that she could use it as a weapon against him—that she had any weapon at all. "There are so few things you want that you can't have, aren't there? Too bad for you I'm one of them."

CHAPTER FIVE

"YOU'VE lost your mind," Jack bit out icily, ordering himself to step away from her—though he did not move so much as an inch. He made his voice even colder, even crueler. She should have frozen where she stood—but instead she seemed to shimmer with more heat than the fire in the fireplace. "I've already had everything you're offering. You're embarrassing yourself."

But she was Larissa Whitney, and he should have remembered that she could not be embarrassed. That she was incapable of feeling such a thing. There was a hard look in her emerald eyes, more like precious stones tonight than he remembered them being before. She only smirked at him, and leaned back against the arm of the sofa, putting that lithe, lush little body of hers on display.

And he, God help him, could not look away. She was as perfect as he remembered. Her skin looked like spun sugar, peaches and cream, and the warm vanilla scent of her rose in the air, making him uncomfortably hard. Ready. He wanted to pull her into his arms. He wanted to suck those pert, dark nipples into his mouth, and lick them until she writhed against him. He wanted to make her climax, screaming his name.

But he wouldn't allow himself to do anything like that, no matter how hard he was. No matter how much he wanted her. She was toxic.

"I'm not embarrassed," she said, her voice so disarmingly, distractingly sweet. Just one more of her lies, he told himself. Harshly. "Isn't this what you wanted? Me—naked and prostrate before you? Begging for your help so you can piously, self-righteously turn me away?" That crook of her lips twisted further, and something seemed to twist in him, too. "Or maybe you don't like to do things halfway," she murmured suggestively, and her delicate hands went to the low-slung fly of her jeans.

"Stop!" The word was out before Jack knew he meant to speak, ringing in the air between them. Her eyes narrowed, and he realized with an uncomfortable start that she was very, very angry.

"I don't understand," she said, her voice too crisp. Too pointed. It made something hard and uncomfortable move through him. "How am I supposed to trap you with my wiles and complete lack of self-respect if my clothes stay on?"

That sat there for a moment between them, ugly

and unobscured. Jack felt his teeth grind against the mounting tension, against his own urge to close the distance between them and finish this conversation in a far more direct manner.

"What do you want, Larissa?" he demanded. Because he could not have what he wanted from her, and if he was the kind of man he was supposed to be, he wouldn't want it. Her.

"I thought you already knew," she threw at him. "I thought you just took great pleasure in telling me. You, on your high horse, because you decided to change your life and everyone played along. Lucky you. It must be nice to breathe such rarified air." She straightened from the couch, all elegant lines and tempting flesh, and made everything worse by stepping even closer, her hands wide at her sides. "Well, here I am, Jack. Prostituting myself. Just as you predicted." Her head tilted to one side. "But if I'm a prostitute, what, I wonder, does that make you?"

"You said I couldn't have you," he reminded her, trying to keep himself from reaching over and putting his hands on her. "And yet now you're half-naked and prostituting yourself? Which is it?"

"You all but called me a whore," she snapped at him. "Yet you're the one who kissed me. You're the one who can't keep his hands to himself. At the end of the day, I'm still the one who walked away from you."

"It would be smarter not to keep reminding me of that," he told her, too softly, denying the kick of temper in his gut. "It's not one of my favorite memories of you." He could pretend as well as she could, he told himself. That he was angry simply about her presence here, in his one sacred space in all the world. That he would feel the same about any other specter of the New York social scene.

"Isn't that what this is all about?" she demanded. Again, that hard, glittering look in her usually sad eyes. "Isn't that what makes you so bound and determined to lord yourself over me? I had the temerity to walk out on the great Jack Endicott Sutton. A dirty, shameless whore like me."

He hated those words. That she would use them, that she meant them. That she believed he thought them. More than that, he had the strangest urge to protect her from them, as if they were blows. He wanted to make her take them back. He didn't know what the source of that feeling was, but it washed over him like another kick of temper.

"I never called you a whore—" he began.

"Didn't you?" Her eyes flashed at him, green fire. And still she stood there so nonchalantly, gloriously half-naked, and he wanted her so badly he ached with it. He found himself drifting closer. She only watched him, a certain sharp amusement and a deeper anger clashing in her gaze. It should not have felt like an aphrodisiac.

"Larissa." His hands bunched into fists at his sides—when he knew he could simply reach over now and cup those small, delectable breasts in his palms. "Put that sweater back on."

"I've worn less than this on the covers of magazines," she said with a sniff, moving her hips in a way that made her whole body sway—and made his mouth run dry. "When did you become such a prude?"

When you walked onto my island, he thought grimly. *When you walked back into my life. I don't even care why you're here, I just—*

But he could not allow himself to finish that thought.

He reached down and scooped up her sweater, holding it out toward her, more or less ordering her to take it from him. The back of his hand brushed the silky skin just south of her collarbone, sending sensation rioting through him. She inhaled, sharply, and he felt it as if she'd used that mouth directly on him.

They stared at each other, the air itself erotic all around them, the tension unbearable.

"Put the damned thing back on or I will do it for you," he said. "And that will not end the way you want it to end. I can promise you that."

She searched his face for a moment. Her mouth flattened into a serious line, and she blinked.

"I can assure you that you have absolutely no idea what I want," she said, but there was a darkness, suddenly, in those changeable eyes. She snatched the black sweater from him, taking care to keep from touching him, he noticed, and then pulled it back over her head with as little warning or fanfare as when she'd removed it.

And then she was looking at him again, warily, that elegant face of hers more appealing, somehow, beneath her newly darkened, newly shortened hair—her cheekbones more pronounced, her mouth more lush. Her eyes more shadowed. He remembered all the things she'd said to him in her inn room earlier, everything he'd dismissed as just so much spinning of her latest tale of woe, designed to pull him in and suck him under. He reminded himself that she was like a riptide, and he had no intention of succumbing. But she looked small and weary, suddenly, swallowed up in that black turtleneck, and he found he could not bear that. He refused to wonder why.

"What happened to you?" he asked quietly.

He had not meant to ask her that. He'd had some complicated idea of revenge and humiliation tonight, hadn't he? Some fantasy that he would show her how little her games worked on him now? He could hardly remember. The fire crackled behind them, and the room seemed smaller. Closer. She smiled, and though it was not that practiced siren's smile, or not quite, it still did not reach her eyes.

"You already know what happened to me," she said softly, that weariness now in her eyes, the curve of her mouth. "The whole world knows what happened to me. It is recorded for posterity, and trotted out again every week or two to sell more papers. My pain makes excellent entertainment."

"Theo," he guessed, and shoved aside the odd pang that he felt when he said the other man's name. "You were with him for a long time." Just about five years, in fact, if his math was as correct as he knew it was. He shoved that aside, too. "Losing him must have been very painful."

"Not in the way you think," she said, and laughed slightly. It was a hollow sound, and she looked away. "He found someone who looked just like me but—crucially—was not me. Not surprisingly, she suits him much better. I don't really blame him. I can't say that I ever appreciated him at all."

He didn't like the way she said that—and couldn't understand why he cared. Why her eyes seemed too big while her mouth seemed too fragile. Or why she seemed small, suddenly. Breakable. *Already broken.*

"Perhaps he is the one who didn't appreciate you," Jack heard himself say—and he was not sure who was more surprised, Larissa or himself.

Her smile was crooked, her green eyes sad again. One shoulder moved in a kind of shrug. "If that's true, it's nobody's fault but mine."

The moment stretched out between them, and Jack found himself reaching out for her, tracing the line of her aristocratic cheekbone, the breathtaking curve of her perfect lips. Something he didn't understand moved through him, confusing him. Heat, yes—all that riot of *need* and *want*—but something else beneath. And all the while she looked at him with eyes like the sea, as if she was only waiting for him to hurt her, too. He hated it.

"I think I'm going to go," she said after a long moment, her voice husky. She produced her Mona Lisa smile, so enigmatic, and Jack decided he hated the very sight of it, too. "Not everyone can say that they stripped for Jack Endicott Sutton in his private Maine retreat. I'll have to add that to my list of most—"

"Stay," he said. He hadn't known he meant to speak. She let her voice trail away, her eyes big and wary. How could she make him feel like the monster in this scenario? "To dinner," he clarified, and smiled, calling on all his charm, all his finesse. She blinked. "I did promise I would feed you, didn't I?"

She let out a little laugh, silvery in the air around them.

"How can I refuse?" she asked lightly.

It was exactly what she'd said over five years ago, he thought as a heat flooded through him, when he'd heeded an urge he'd never had before—not with her, at any rate—and asked her to leave that party with him. He couldn't remember, now, who had thrown that party or even if it had been for one of the many charities he supported with his presence and checkbook, as was expected of members of his social circle. All he could remember was how he'd touched her, kissed her. He remembered the feel of her skin beneath his fingers, the heat of her decadent mouth. He remembered the wild passion, the intense need that had nearly taken him out at the knees. Touching Larissa was like diving into the heart of a volcano, and he'd loved it. The rush. The danger. Adrenaline and desire.

He had known her for years. He was not one to waste his time reading trashy fiction in the gutter press, not even back then when he'd starred in so many lurid fantasies presented as fact—but even so, he would have to have been entombed underground somewhere not to recognize that Larissa Whitney was the It Girl of their time. Her every word, action, outfit and hairstyle scrutinized, criticized and then ruthlessly copied. He'd been surprised to find that she was so sharp, so funny.

She'd made him laugh when he'd been resigned to another night of desperate tedium. Then they'd danced together on a rooftop with all of Manhattan laid out at their feet, and touching her had felt like burning alive. His mother had just died, he'd been reeling from a loss he could hardly make sense of nor admit, and somehow, Larissa Whitney had seemed like a touchstone. An anchor to the world, though not, perhaps, of it. She was the only thing that had broken through his numbness, his despair, like a bright shining lighthouse on the edge of a dangerous cliff.

"Come with me," he'd said. Had he ordered her or pleaded with her? His memory was unreliable on that point.

She'd had her arms locked around his neck, those perfect small breasts pressed against him like twin points of flame, and her green eyes had seemed to sear right through him. He'd thought she was magical. She'd felt like some kind of spell, her body an enchantment against his, and he'd felt like his own kind of magic holding her that close, with the whole city made up of interlocking ropes of light spread out behind her and below her like a labyrinth.

She'd laughed as if every part of that moment delighted her, as if he'd delighted her even more, straight down to the soles of her expertly, expensively-shod feet. She hadn't asked him where he wanted to go, or what he'd wanted to do. She hadn't played any of those games. He'd thought she wasn't playing any games at all. She'd leaned closer then, and she'd pressed her full lips to his, a cool challenge. A hint. Like a deep, consuming flame. Like destiny, he'd thought.

"How can I refuse?" she'd asked in that light, easy voice of hers, a sweet whisper in his ear.

He'd felt it like a thunderbolt.

But if she remembered that, Jack thought, searching her face, he saw no sign of it now. Her face was smooth as glass, and perhaps he only imagined that there were things to be learned still in the darkness of her unreadable eyes. Perhaps he simply wanted that to be true.

Perhaps he was a far greater fool than he had previously believed.

He led her through to the back of the house, where the original kitchen had long since been remodeled to suit more modern tastes. He walked over to the subzero refrigerator and began pulling things out of it, setting them out on the counter.

"You cook?" He could hear the laughter in her voice, though when he looked over his shoulder at her, her eyes were veiled. She stood by the rough-hewn wood table, running her fingers over the nooks and crannies.

"I value my privacy," he said with a shrug. "That means no staff and no deliveries, even if there was any place that delivered out here." He waited until her eyes rose to meet his. "And as I am not feral, that means that yes, I cook."

"The Manhattan glitterati would be so distraught if they had any idea that you were so competent," she said, moving toward him, a smile flirting with her mouth. "It would destroy whole fantasies about how much work a man like you must be."

"But it depends on what you consider onerous," he said, rummaging through the well-stocked shelves of the whitewashed cupboard above him. "Having thoughts that do not revolve around parties and shopping? Having a purpose in life beyond depleting the family fortune? Is that too much work?"

"You know that it is," Larissa said, once again with that thread of laughter woven through her voice.

She moved to stand next to him, and Jack had the strangest sensation, like some kind of déjà vu. As if she belonged there, standing close to him like this, in a kitchen of all places. In *this* kitchen. As if this was their life. As if they shared something more than that unforgettable, unquenchable fire. Where did *that* come from?

She frowned down at the items he'd laid out on the counter, wrinkling her fine nose as he pulled dry pasta from a canister in the overhead cupboard. He'd put out a few sausages. Tomatoes and basil. A hunk of good cheese and a bulb of garlic.

She glanced at him then, and he had the oddest feeling that she'd seen it too, that almost-hallucination. That fantasy of a life he couldn't even begin to imagine. Not really. He wanted Larissa; perhaps he always had. But that was just sex. Explosive, white-hot sex that he'd briefly mistaken for something more emotional during the darkest period of his life. It was only that she was here, he assured himself, in Scatteree Pines. In this house, where no one from his other world was ever allowed to come. That was what made him think of things he knew he shouldn't—didn't—want.

"I'll chop the garlic," she offered.

It was so incongruous. And yet…it was as if she fit. As if that odd feeling was still working its way through him. He told himself it was just the rain, just the storm. Making the very shadows seem meaningful when they were not.

"I'm not at all sure how I feel about you brandishing a knife in my kitchen," he said. And she smiled. It wasn't that fake smile of hers, that mysterious bit of nothing she trotted out for the masses. This smile showed the faintest hint of a dimple in her cheek, and the flash of her teeth. He even saw it in the gleam of gold that warmed the green of her eyes. That was real, he thought, dazed by the punch of it, the way it electrified him. *He'd just seen the real Larissa.*

Something warm moved through him then, and that was when he was sure of it: he should never have invited this woman here. Ever. He should have pretended he hadn't seen her in that bar, and gone about his business. But he had always had a regrettable weakness where Larissa Whitney was concerned. What was one more bit of proof?

It was like a dream.

Larissa chopped garlic and basil, then cut into the plump tomatoes. Olive oil sizzled in a cast-iron pan on the big stove top, and the kitchen seemed to glow with warmth and laughter, as if such things shone down from the walls. As if they had been trapped there over the course of long, happy years, and blossomed at the rich scent of garlic and the leftover summer brashness of the basil.

Jack whipped things together in a selection of pans with a briskness that spoke of long practice, then finally poured the mixture of ingredients over the hot, fresh pasta. Larissa picked up the pasta bowls without being asked and took them over to the table, as if they'd choreographed it. As if they'd performed this simple, shared ritual a thousand times before. It occurred to her, with a little thump of shock, that this was the most intimate she had ever been with anyone. Much less a man.

The realization made a shiver run through her. She felt as if the floor beneath her feet was suddenly precarious.

"That's not the first time you've chopped vegetables, clearly," Jack observed, in that deceptively casual way of his that made her suspect he was looking for clues. Did he think she was some great mystery he felt called upon to solve? Or was he merely looking for confirmation of existing prejudices? In her experience, it was always one or the other. And it never ended well.

But tonight, she couldn't let herself think of that, not in the way she should. Not while the kitchen was so bright and cheery, holding the storm and the dark at bay. Not while she could smell garlic and basil in the air, and not when she sat at a simple wooden table to eat a meal she'd helped prepare, with a man who looked the way she'd always dreamed a man—*her* man—would look, should she ever find one of those.

If she took this moment out of time—forgot what came before, what had just happened in the sitting room—maybe, just this once, she wouldn't have to pretend. Maybe she could simply, truly enjoy herself.

"I haven't cooked anything in longer than I can remember," she started to say, and then cut herself off—sure, somehow, that she had revealed too much. That he would call her *poor little rich girl* or something worse and she would deserve it, and she wasn't sure she could handle the necessary self-recrimination just now. But he only gazed at her, his beautiful face inscrutable, his dark eyes so much more compelling than they should be. She swallowed. She should know better than to let this night, this man, get to her. She should be more realistic. She knew she should.

"My mother had a housekeeper at her home in France," she said as she settled herself in the heavy wooden chair across from him. She pulled the coarse linen napkin onto her lap. "Her name was Hilaire and she was ferocious. More a displaced tyrant than an employee."

She gazed at the wide bowls in front of them, the ceramic surfaces gleaming with the bright blues and joyful yellows of Provence. It almost felt as if she was tucked away in the château across the Atlantic with her silent, perpetually unwell mother, surrounded on all sides by plane trees, azure skies and fields of lavender. She could almost hear Hilaire's ill-tempered muttering as she forced spoiled, defiant Larissa to perform any chores she deemed suitable, and the more menial, the better. They were some of her favorite memories, though Larissa knew better to admit such things aloud. People always got the wrong impression.

But when she looked up, she saw only the deep brown of Jack's eyes, and the way he lounged there, his big, powerful body so relaxed in that chair, his elegant fingers toying with his wineglass. Why that should make her feel at ease in response, she was afraid to examine.

"She believed that every woman should know how to prepare a decent meal," Larissa said.

She shrugged out of habit, always so quick to pretend that these things meant nothing to her. That she had not looked upon those endless hours in the airless kitchen, making inevitable messes that would cause Hilaire to unleash a torrent of abrasive French, as the highlights of her childhood. At least someone, somewhere, had cared enough to correct her, to show her how to improve. Later, she would hate the way leaving Provence made her feel—though she would never admit that to herself in so many words—and so she'd stopped going. And in time, Hilaire had left her mother's employ, and Larissa had only visited the château when she grew bored with the yachts cluttering up the St. Tropez harbor or with the celebrity-infested commotion of Cannes. And so her life had remained empty, uncluttered. Anesthetized.

Those could not be tears that pricked the back of her eyes.

Jack smiled slightly, and picked up his fork.

"My mother felt the same," he said, his voice low. As if he was as wary of this—this intimacy—as she was. "She said that no son of hers would go through life unable to care for himself in the most basic way." His smile deepened, though he aimed it at the food before them, and Larissa felt the slightest pang. She wondered what it would be like to be what caused that wistful smile, what called it forth. He looked at her after a moment, that smile more guarded. "She was an Endicott through and through, just like my grandfather. The 'Sutton excesses' made her uncomfortable."

"What about you?" Larissa asked. "You fall somewhere in between the Puritan Endicotts and the profligate Suttons, don't you?"

She remembered the younger Jack, the careless Jack. The famous playboy Jack. He'd driven impossibly expensive cars, had dropped unimaginable sums of money on forgettable evenings. He'd been like all the rest of them. Their peers. Their "friends." She took a bite of the pasta, sighing happily as the rich flavors washed into her, chasing away the damp, the cold. The fight.

He flashed that devastating smile at her, the one that had made him so beloved, America's most eligible bachelor. She had to look away from all that shine, and told herself she didn't know why.

"People have to change, Larissa," he said, in an

odd tone. When she looked back at him, however, his expression was shuttered. "What other choice do they have?"

"Most people never change," she countered, with a shrug that felt too sharp. "Most people balk at the slightest suggestion that they should. Most people will go to great and dizzying lengths to make sure that absolutely nothing changes, ever. Themselves, their lives. Nothing."

"Then they are no better than children," Jack said dismissively. He stabbed at his pasta, and she could not help but admire the leashed ferocity in him, the controlled power. She felt too much these days, and far more than that when she was with him. Far too much. "An adult must take responsibility for himself. He must do what is expected of him. If that requires change, so be it. It is called growing up. It is his duty."

"It's a very unusual person who simply wakes up one morning and decides, apropos of nothing, to change their life," she said, picking her words carefully, still thinking she could protect herself somehow from the things she could not help but feel. "I suspect that sweeping personal change is more often preceded by some catastrophic personal event. Because why would anyone risk it, otherwise? It's too painful." She took another bite, chewed it thoughtfully. "And of course, no one supports change. Everyone around you will fight tooth and nail to keep you in exactly the box they put you in, much too afraid of what it might mean to let you go free. No one ever changes, if they can avoid it. No one."

He didn't say anything for a moment, studying her from across the table. And then he blinked, and the tension seemed to ease again somehow, like the tides. They talked of other things. The island's history. His own summers here as a boy. Innocuous subjects, until they had both eaten their fill. Larissa carried their bowls to the deep sink and when she turned, found him close behind her. Too close. He leaned in, bracing himself with a hand on either side of her, caging her between his strong arms.

She knew she should do something. Scream. Run. Object, at the very least. But she only stared, while her blood seemed to turn into molten lava beneath her skin.

"Have you changed, Larissa?" he asked softly, a half smile on his mouth though his brown eyes were serious. "Is that what you've been trying to tell me?"

All of her anxiety and fear rushed back into her then, shaking her. How could she have forgotten what a threat this man was? How had she managed to shove that aside? Had the unexpected— and highly unlikely—fantasy of domestic bliss completely addled her? Or was it the surprising memories of her time in Provence, that she normally kept as hidden away as possible?

"I don't make pronouncements about whether I've changed," she said, tilting her head back to look him in the eye. Pretending she felt strong. "How pompous. Have you ever heard someone make an announcement like that without then proving—usually shortly thereafter—that they hadn't changed at all?"

"Rarely," he said. But his gaze was trained on her mouth and darkening by the moment. "But then, not everyone has quite as far to go as you do, do they?"

There was some part of her that wanted to hate him for that comment, so snide and so off-handed—and part of her did hate him for it. It was the same part that curled up into a tight ball and wondered how she had ever let her defenses down, how she had ever given him the opportunity to hurt her. Because she'd expected more, somehow, after the way this odd evening had gone. That was her mistake. She'd expected better from him, from this. More fool, she. Would she never learn?

"No, of course not," she said, trying desperately to shove her walls back into place. Trying to prop them up again, keep him out somehow. "I am the poster child for ruin. Thank you for reminding me."

Why should she feel as if her usually hard, impenetrable defenses had been broken, somehow? Chipped? From one simple dinner? She couldn't even call this strange interlude an act of kindness on his part—it had been much more a simple lack of active malice. Was that all it took to make her lose her head? Was she that pathetic?

She knew, of course, that she was. Or that it was Jack who soothed her into a false sense of security, who made her forget herself. Who made her want to believe in fantasies—who made her remember too much, expose herself too much and *feel* too much. Hadn't she run from exactly that five years ago? Hadn't she known better even then? On some level, hadn't it been that weekend with Jack that had inspired her to walk, eyes wide open, into a loveless, controllably numb engagement to Theo?

"Why do I want to believe all the things you're saying tonight, Larissa?" His voice was a whisper, a low rasp of sound, and she shouldn't have felt it like a caress. She shouldn't have felt it trace patterns of swirling heat down her arms, across her belly, and below. He shifted closer, and she was *aware* of him with every cell of her body. Aware of his height, the strength and width of his shoulders, the hard cage of his powerful chest. Aware of his beautiful mouth, his knowing gaze, too close to hers. "And if you're not who I think you are, why don't you defend yourself?"

She laughed slightly, but it was a blocking maneuver more than any kind of humor. "Never defend, never explain," she said airily, though the light tone cost her. "Didn't someone famous say that?"

"If you can't defend," he urged her, his mouth so close, too close, not nearly close enough, "then you really should explain. There's only the two of us here. No one will know but me."

"And me," Larissa replied. The crazy part was that she wanted to tell him. She wanted to explain everything to him, to share it all with him. What kind of insanity was that? And to what end? Did she think he could save her somehow? He was far more likely to ridicule her. And on some level she knew that this time she had to save herself, whatever that might look like. Whatever it took.

"Larissa…" He said her name like it was a song. A curse. His strong hands cupped her face, then slid back to bury themselves in her hair. She felt a kind of drumbeat roll through her, low and deep, insistent.

She was so afraid of this man. And at the same time, she'd never felt more awake. More alive. He made her feel that way. He always had. He made her *feel*.

"If you live any kind of complicated life," she said, whispering, her eyes glued to his, her skin shrinking over her bones, too small and too hot for her own body, "there will be people who hate you, and there's nothing you can do to change their minds." His eyes were so dark. So magnetic. She felt as if she could drown in them—as if she already had. "You can only move forward, and try to cause less damage. Less harm. What else is there to do?"

"Less damage?" he echoed. His fingers flexed against her scalp, making her press into him. His words seemed to caress her mouth. "Less harm? What does that even look like for someone like you?"

And she couldn't seem to help herself. She couldn't seem to do what she knew she should. She couldn't make herself step away, put space between them, leave. She had always been so weak, so unable to resist temptation. And Jack Sutton was the greatest temptation of all, even when he hurt her.

She was so tired of self-examination, of fearlessly looking at her own reflection, of taking honest stock of what she'd made of herself. And she had always been so weak for him. Always. She was still.

Larissa pushed up on her toes, closed the breath of space between them, accepted that she was damned, and fit her mouth to his.

CHAPTER SIX

THE kiss exploded all around her, through her. Need punched into her as she tasted him, as he angled his head to fully capture her mouth, his hands holding her fast as he took her mouth with his. And again. And then again.

It was too much. It would never be enough.

Larissa wanted to be closer, to touch him, to feel him under her hands. She pushed his sweater out of the way, her fingers trembling with excitement, to feel his rock-hard abdomen under her palms. The heat of his skin was like a burst of fire, singeing her, blasting through her.

He muttered her name, a curse or a prayer and she didn't care which, and then shifted to lift her up and settle her on the lip of the sink. She hardly noticed; she just draped her legs over his hips and lost herself in the fit of him against her, the way their bodies seemed to ignite on contact. And the sweet insanity of his hot mouth as it tasted her, taught her, took her.

She was caught in the tumble of memories she'd held at bay for so long, all of them chasing each other and fusing, somehow, with the present, making his kiss that much hotter, her heart beat that much harder. She saw them together in her head, skin slick and so much pleasure, and when she focused on *now* his hands were on her body and she couldn't seem to catch her breath. He was dark and wicked and she could do nothing but burn, molten-hot and then hotter still.

There was some part of her, still, that knew better. That knew what a terrible mistake this was—and suspected there would be a harsh price to pay for giving in to this particular temptation—but she didn't care. She couldn't bring herself to care—she couldn't let herself. His clever lips drifted from her mouth to her jawline, leaving a trail of fire as he went, and she simply couldn't bring herself to stop it. She couldn't make herself do it. She was still so weak, after everything she'd been through.

She had always been the most foolish of creatures, so hell-bent on her own destruction, hadn't she? At least here, now, with Jack, she was almost convinced that touching him like this—tasting him—was worth whatever pain would come later. He took her mouth again in that powerful, commanding way and Larissa had the flashing, dizzying thought that it was worth anything at all.

So instead of beating herself up any further over things she wasn't going to change—not tonight, not now—she moved closer. She reached down and tugged on the hem of his sweater, urging him to pull it up and over his head. He complied with a lazy masculine grace, shrugging it from his smooth, strong shoulders, and Larissa let out a soft sigh. It was as if he'd been carved from marble, yet he felt like hot, smooth satin beneath her greedy hands. He was glorious.

He will wreck you, that little voice whispered. But she was already wrecked in all the ways that mattered, wasn't she? And she couldn't see why she should deny herself this, why she should punish herself more than she already had, for something that felt as inevitable as the rain that drummed against the windows behind her. As inescapable. As if his mouth against hers had been a foregone conclusion the moment she'd looked up and seen him standing there in the door of that bar, weather all around him.

Maybe it had been inevitable that they would end up this way since that weekend five years ago. Larissa just couldn't bring herself to regret that, not when he tasted like magic and he moved against her as though they were both made of that ache, that heat.

His hands moved down her back, managing to sear into her despite the heavy sweater she wore.

Then they moved to her legs, holding her thighs so that she could feel his warmth through the faded denim. He shifted, pulling her legs higher over his hips, pressing his hardness tight against the core of her. Larissa felt a wave crash over her, through her—some potent mix of lust, need, fire.

He inhaled sharply; Larissa gasped aloud.

His chest was like a wall in front of her, hard and unyielding, and Larissa dropped her head forward. She tasted him, salt and man, and then followed the distracting lines of his defined muscles before pressing her mouth against that valley between his pectorals. He was lean and athletic, all rip-cord strength and smooth, confident power. *Perfect,* she chanted somewhere deep inside, like a prayer to the gods she'd disappointed long ago. *This man is perfect.*

"You are overdressed," he said, his voice a low thread of sound in the quiet room. It hummed with the same need that coursed through her, and made her feel like someone else. Made her imagine she could be whoever this was, this woman he held in his hands who turned so very bright with his touch. Brighter than she'd ever been before—when she'd spent so many years believing she'd only ever be the same shade of gray. Yet here, with him, she felt herself glow. Shine. She leaned back slightly, their hips still flush against each other, and studied his face.

His cheekbones seemed sharper somehow, as if desire rendered them more prominent, and his dark eyes were nearly black with passion. They glittered down at her, fierce and demanding. An answering drumbeat kicked up inside her skin, a thick pulse that made her heart skip and a heaviness coil low in her belly. She could not remember ever wanting anyone or anything as much as she wanted this man. Not five years ago, not now.

Without looking away from him, Larissa lifted her arms over her head, let her lips crook slightly, imperiously, and waited. Jack's mouth pulled into something too edgy to be a smile. His dark eyes caught fire. An echoing shiver raced down Larissa's back, then became a low and insistent pulse between her legs.

He took the bottom of her sweater in his big hands and began to pull it up, inch by agonizing inch. Slowly, carefully, bit by bit, he bared her skin to the cooler air of the kitchen. Punishing her, she was suddenly convinced, for her little half-naked show earlier. With a gentleness that belied the stark hunger stamped across his face, he tugged it over her head and then discarded it, his attention immediately drawn to the breasts he'd finally revealed. He let out a breath, low and jagged, that danced over her skin and made her nipples draw tight. Slowly, as if in some kind of awe, he cupped a breast in each hard palm, testing them against his heat, his strength. His thumbs dragged over each peak, and she arched helplessly against him, pressing her breasts more fully into his hands as the exquisite pleasure threatened to spiral out of control.

Then he bent down and sucked one tight, hard nipple into his mouth, and Larissa lost herself completely. Her head fell back and she could only moan out her pleasure.

She clung to him as the world spun around, as she spun around—and she was only vaguely conscious of the fact he was actually lifting her. She could only concentrate on the wicked perfection of his mouth on her breast, and the wild, consuming heat that pulled tighter and tighter in her core.

"Hold on," he muttered urgently, pulling his mouth away and lifting her higher against him. Larissa wound her arms around his neck and her legs tight around his waist and gloried in the slide of her skin against his, his heat against hers, and the way each step he took rocked him harder and tighter against her very center.

She was flat on her back before she realized what he was doing, and it took her longer than it should have to realize he'd simply laid her down on the table, spread out before him like his own, personal feast.

He loomed over her, beautiful and dark, propping himself up on his hands as he let his gaze travel down the length of her torso. He straightened, letting his hands move to her legs, then carefully smoothed them down one of her gleaming black boots before he gently tugged it off. Larissa registered the thunk of it against the kitchen floor, but he was already on to the other one, the slightest frown between his brows, as if undressing her was a task that required his fiercest concentration.

So she could do nothing when his hands moved to the button of her jeans but lift her hips and let him peel them down her legs, baring her entirely to his gaze, save the tiny scrap of scarlet that covered her sex.

For a moment, he only looked at her, his dark eyes burning that deep, passionate black, that same rough hunger that beat in her making his face seem nearly grim. She felt weak, wild. Deliciously wet. She felt that current running through her again, electric and demanding, making her feel as if her body was not her own. That she had not lived in five long years, not since he'd last had his hands, his mouth, on her. That there was only this. That there could never be, had never been, anything but Jack.

It was too much to bear, too much to survive intact. She was shaken by the depth of her own longing, her own desperation. All these *feelings*. It was like a tidal wave—sensation after sensation crashing over her, threatening to drown her. She could hardly take it all in. She felt a restlessness wind through her—a kind of sensual panic, and knew she had to move, or it might well burn her alive. She sat up, pulling him closer to her by the waistband of his jeans, trembling slightly at the feel of his hair-roughened skin against the back of her fingers, and the intense heat of his body.

This was too much. *He* was too much.

But she couldn't seem to stop. She didn't *want* to stop. Something she would no doubt castigate herself for…but later. *Later.*

He looked down at her, and the frank hunger and sensual heat in his dark gaze made her ache. She kept her eyes on his as she undid the button of his jeans, and then slowly pulled the zipper down, moving carefully over his impressive hardness. She could hear the storm against the windows and the wind howl around the sides of the house as if it came from far away. But here, now, there was only the sound of his breath, and her own, and then the smooth, hard length of him in her hands. Only him. Only Jack.

Too much. Never enough.

"Not now," he said, as if the words hurt him. She could hardly understand what he was saying, so intent was she on relearning the shape of him. She swayed closer, as if to pull him into her mouth, to truly taste him, and she heard his slight groan as he stopped her.

He pulled her hands away from him, and leaned down to catch her mouth with his, his kiss scalding hot, demanding. Larissa fell back and he followed, pulling her hips toward him down the length of the table. Propping himself up on one arm, he continued to kiss her, deeper and with more raw command, as his other hand traced the shallow indentation of her belly button, then moved farther south. He pulled the scrap of scarlet to the side, and then slipped his long fingers into the wet heat beneath.

Finally. *Fire.* Larissa arched against his hand, her mind spinning out, dizzy and desperate.

"Jack…" she managed to say, and it was like throwing kerosene on an already out-of-control blaze. She felt his focus sharpen, as his hands traced her secret curves, then a long finger tested her entrance. Then two. She shuddered in anticipation, in joy, in the helpless wonder, the enormity, of what he made her feel.

He moved closer, the blunt head of him pressed up against her, so very close, and then—impossibly—he stopped. He looked at her.

Just looked at her. As if he was trying to see… everything.

She was nearly mindless. Nearly. She felt that dark, nearly black gaze from the top of her head to the tips of her toes. Inside and out. It was as if he was already deep within her, had already claimed her. Changed her. And she knew, in the way she always had, that there was nothing about this man that could ever be taken lightly. That he demanded too much, and would take too much, and there was no way around that simple, salient truth.

But the other truth was that her desire for him was like a poison in her blood, turning her inside out, alive and sharp and *now*. She hooked her legs around his hips, swiveled hers, and pulled him into her.

Too much. Never, ever enough.

He slid all the way home, hard and sure, and she burst into a shower of light all around him.

He waited until she opened her eyes again, those sea-green depths shot through with gold, dazed as she slowly focused on him, and then, only then, he began to move.

She was even more perfect than he'd remembered, than he'd dreamed all these years. Her soft curves, her lithe body, her dangerously addictive mouth. The small sounds she began to make in the back of her throat as he set a slow, steady pace. The scent of vanilla hung in the air between them, tempting him, teasing him, making him move faster, deeper.

He built her up again, using his hands and his tongue and his mouth. He played with her, with that masterpiece of a body that he'd never expected he'd touch again, laid out before him, his to command. Her hips rose to meet his, her nails dug into his back, and she clung to him, urging him on.

He wanted her too badly. He wanted all of her. He reached between them, unerringly finding the very center of her pleasure, and stroked her, even as he kept up his demanding pace. He felt her tense again, her muscles clenching his, her mouth against his skin.

And then, finally, she screamed out his name and he followed her, tumbling over the edge into oblivion.

When he could breathe again, he pulled back from her so he could study that beautiful face of hers. Trying, once again and with as little hope of success, to figure out what went on behind those perfect bones, that flawless skin. She lay sprawled across the kitchen table like some kind of banquet, her skin flushed a light shade of rose, her arms stretched above her head in total abandon.

God, she was beautiful. The most beautiful thing he'd ever seen.

It made him harden again. It made him want her as if he hadn't just had her. It made him want things he'd told himself were part and parcel of that darkness five years ago, things he'd told himself had never been real.

But she was real, and she was here. And for this moment, at least, she was his.

He told himself that kick he felt in his chest was anticipation for the night ahead, nothing more.

Jack stepped back and refastened the jeans he'd never managed to fully remove, then adjusted the scrap of scarlet between her legs, putting it back into place. Larissa stirred slightly, though her eyes stayed closed. She looked…soft. Almost vulnerable. He felt something move through him, and told himself he had no idea what it was. None at all.

He didn't question his actions then, he just swept her up and into his arms. He was halfway up the stairs before her eyes opened, fixing on him in that solemn, disarming way of hers.

"Don't argue," he told her gruffly, feeling something too close to emotional, something much too raw. Explosive. Did he expect her to argue with him? Did he want her to argue? Did he fear it? "You're staying."

She pulled her lower lip between her teeth and her green eyes looked guarded, suddenly, but she didn't say a word.

He carried her into the sprawling suite at the top of the stairs, his favorite in the house. It took over the front of the second story and looked out over the vastness of the sea from three side-by-side bay windows that stood at proud attention on the outside wall. Inside, he moved to the big, wrought-iron four-poster bed that sat in the center of the room, piled high with snowy white linens, and deposited her in the middle of it.

Because she was Larissa Whitney, she showed no evidence of any second thoughts or regrets, or even any acknowledgment that it was far chillier upstairs than it had been in the kitchen. Instead, she closed her eyes again and stretched out like a cat, her lithe body so smooth, so endlessly fascinating, spread out on the soft, old quilt.

Mine, he thought. It rang in him like the low toll of the island's old church bells, deep and true, but he didn't let himself worry about what that might mean. It didn't matter. It couldn't.

He didn't hesitate. He didn't think it through. He moved to sit next to her, opening a drawer in the chest that stood next to the bed, the repository of some thirty summers, including the long-ago summers when he'd put on plays to amuse his mother. Larissa was warm next to him, vanilla and musk, and he could not bring himself to regret what he was about to do. Or even question it. He pulled out the pair of heavy steel handcuffs he'd once used as part of a costume, clicked one circle tight around her wrist, and attached the other to the scrolled-iron headboard.

Her eyes opened slowly. Perhaps too slowly, too deliberately. She blinked, though she showed no particular sign of alarm, and then she tested the handcuff against the iron scrollwork, pulling on it slightly before letting her arm rest back against the pillows.

"Kinky," she said mildly. Her gaze moved to his, clear and faintly amused. "And me without my safe word."

"I don't want you to get any ideas," Jack said, his voice rough in the stillness of the room.

"Says the man who just cuffed me to his four-poster bed." Her voice was dry.

"About leaving without telling me." His gaze drilled into hers. "Like the last time."

Her expression didn't change, but he felt the air around them shimmer slightly with the tension that never quite disappeared. She moved her arm, letting the steel clank against iron. Her chin lifted.

"Some men might simply have asked," she said quietly.

"I'm not 'some men,'" he said in the same tone. He moved to sprawl next to her, tracing a line down between those pert breasts with his index finger, pleased to feel that telltale shiver move through her. "And you are certainly not 'some women,' Larissa."

She only looked at him for a moment, that gaze of hers so serious, and still so sad, despite the glaze of passion that deepened whenever he moved his hand against her.

"What kind of woman am I?" she asked, her

voice hardly more than a whisper, and he had the strangest sensation that despite the way she lounged there without an apparent care in the world, as if she routinely found herself almost entirely naked and restrained to various items of furniture, that question cost her. That the answer meant something to her.

He couldn't let himself think about that, either.

He would marry the kind of woman his grandfather approved of, safe and dutiful and boring, who would not remind him of the sea. He would build a life with her, an adult life made of obligation and responsibility, and he would not feel like this again, this roller coaster of desire and a kind of fury, this pounding need to bury himself inside Larissa. He told himself that was what he wanted. What he desired above all else.

But right now, tonight, his duty seemed a far-off thing. There was only this woman stretched out in his bed, waiting for him, flushed and near enough to naked.

"At the moment," he said quietly, intently, the words sounding like a promise he knew better than to make, and had no intention of keeping, "you are mine."

CHAPTER SEVEN

HE RELEASED her from the handcuffs much later that long and breathtakingly intense night, but the hold he kept on her, Larissa thought many days later when she was still on the island and still deep under his spell—was proving much harder to break.

She had woken the following morning feeling bruised—and not physically, which she imagined might have been easier to deal with, all things considered. Physically, though, she'd felt wonderful. More than wonderful—she'd felt *alive*. Vibrant. As if she'd finally understood, after all this time, what her body had been made to do, though she'd tried not to think of it that way.

No, the bruises she'd sustained were of the emotional variety, and Larissa had wanted only to hurry back to her tiny room at the inn, bury herself in the deep and forgiving bath, and try her best not to poke at them. She'd eased herself out from under the delicious weight of Jack's heavy arm, and had moved to the edge of the bed. She'd told herself that her trepidation was only because it was a cold morning, with the rain still beating down against the bay windows that allowed in only a thin, weak light to indicate the night had passed. It was chilly and wet, and she'd known she had to walk all the way to the kitchen to locate her clothes. That, surely, had been reason enough to want to stay in the bed.

But then his hand had snaked out and his arm had wrapped around her waist, capturing her that easily. Not that she'd put up much of a fight. Or any fight. She'd been too busy repressing the deep sigh of contentment that threatened to spill out, just because he'd been touching her again.

Her weakness, she'd told herself then, was truly astonishing. There was so much she'd needed to think about, to come to terms with. The night before had blazed inside her, neon and vivid, and she'd not been at all certain she was the same person she'd been the day before. She'd had no idea who she might have become.

But even so, all she'd wanted to do was lean into him, lose herself in him, as if none of that mattered when he was near.

There would be time for that later, she'd promised herself. When the storm passed, when the smoke from this particular fire cleared. When sanity reasserted itself. She'd deal with it later. She'd have to.

"Do I have to chain you to the bed again?" he'd asked, his voice thick with sleep and far too appealing, dancing down her spine like a touch, like his clever, demanding hands.

"Are you asking for permission this time?" She'd had to force her voice to sound light. He'd tugged on her, gently, until she'd had no choice but to fall back against him, and she'd sighed involuntarily when he'd tucked her back into the heat of his chest, his mouth moving along her neck to tease the tender skin below her ear.

She'd felt him all around her, holding her—his hard chest and his strong thighs behind her, and the evidence of his unquenchable desire stirring against her bottom. He should not have felt so good, she'd told herself with something too close to despair. The rough silk of his skin next to hers should not have made her quiver in delight. She should have been done with him after the night they'd shared. She should have thrown off his arm and walked away. For sheer self-preservation, if nothing else.

But instead Larissa had tilted back her head and met his lips, tasting him as if the desire that flared so easily, so wildly, between them was something other than destructive. As if it might sanctify her somehow, instead of ripping her apart.

"Stay," he'd murmured against her mouth, then turned his attention back to her neck, his hand moving to cup her breast, sending arrows of sensation spiraling through her. "For breakfast."

"I don't eat breakfast," she'd managed to reply, her voice breathy in the morning air as once again her body shook for him, melted against him, did exactly as he'd bade it.

He'd moved over her then, his beautiful face taut with sensual hunger, his eyes much too aware, then twisted his hips and slid deep into her in one smooth, devastating thrust.

She should not have loved that, gloried in it, but she did.

"We'll have to come up with something else to do, then," he'd said roughly against her neck, her mouth.

And then he'd started to move, and she'd stopped thinking for a long, long while.

He hadn't proved any more interested in her leaving throughout the whole of that day and into the next. After an abbreviated walk in the woods a few days after that—an attempt at getting out of the house which had ended with Larissa gripping on to one of the ghostly white birch trees while Jack took her with knee-weakening finesse from behind, his mouth against the back of her neck while he braced himself with one arm on the same tree, whispering things she was afraid to listen to too closely—he'd packed her into his SUV. She had still been shaking from the after-effects of the shattering climax he'd just given her, no matter how hard she'd tried to pretend she'd been unaffected.

He'd driven into the village without further comment, though she'd been able to feel the ever-present tension that simmered beneath the silence, and he had led her to her room in the attic of the small inn. She'd walked in her door, looked around the cheerful little room, and had had the sudden, unreasonably terrifying suspicion that he was going to leave her. Just that easily, she'd thought, and while she was still too disarmed from his lovemaking to do anything but stand there and watch him do it.

And it would be no more than what she deserved, she'd told herself sternly then, for being such a damned fool where this man was concerned. *How did you think this would end?* she'd asked herself incredulously.

"Pack your things," he'd said after a long, too-quiet moment, his brown eyes cool again, once more unreadable. That strange tension had seemed to pull tight then, cinching her around the chest and waist like a particularly vicious corset. But she'd forced herself to breathe. Somehow.

"Has the ferry come?" she'd asked, proud of the

way her voice remained steady, calm. As if she hadn't been able to muster up the strength to care. As if nothing that had been about to happen could possibly affect her one way or the other. As if she couldn't still feel the way he'd moved between her legs, so powerful, so devastating. "Are you tossing me off your island, just as you promised?"

She hadn't liked the way he'd looked at her then, a certain assessment moving through those far-too-discerning eyes, across that fascinating face. His head had tilted slightly to one side as he'd regarded her, as if she was a problem he planned to solve. He'd been the very picture of powerful indolence, one shoulder propped against the door as if he was completely relaxed, but she'd known better than to believe it. She'd certainly known better than to relax her own guard.

"Is that what you want?" he'd asked, his voice, she'd thought, carefully blank. She'd wanted that to mean things it couldn't. She'd wanted that caution to indicate some great, hidden wealth of emotion. She'd wanted too much, as usual. "The next ferry to safety and sanity?"

She'd laughed slightly, defensively, wrapping her arms around herself and not caring what he might read into it. She'd tried not to notice that she was still wearing one of the bulky sweaters he'd given her, telling her they had been his when he was a boy. She'd forbidden herself from remembering what Jack had been like way back when, so lean and young and bathed in effortless gold. Wearing his old clothes, she'd chastised herself then, should feel like nothing more than a convenience. Not like some kind of connection.

"I was under the impression it went to Bar Harbor," she'd said dryly. "Are safety and sanity separate stops along the same route?"

He'd only watched her for another moment, but the fact he'd stayed so still—like some kind of deadly predator moments before the attack—had made her pulse pound in her temples, her neck, her wrists.

"I'm beginning to understand this little act of yours," he'd said, in that suspiciously casual tone that she'd realized, belatedly, was Jack at his most lethal. She'd felt a trickle of something like foreboding ease down her back. "You answer every question with another question, never letting anyone suspect your actual feelings or wishes. And the world takes it at face value, don't they? No one ever talks about how quick you must be, how agile, to do this so often and so well."

She'd hated him in that moment—hated the way he'd looked at her, as if he'd been able to read her like a particularly simple children's book. As if she'd telegraphed her every thought to him and he was lazily dissecting each and every one of them.

"No one talks about you much at all," she'd replied with sweet, false sincerity. "Not anymore. The perils of becoming tediously domesticated when you used to be *the* Jack Endicott Sutton."

His dark eyes had narrowed, and she'd thought he'd tensed, but if he had, he'd quickly suppressed it. He'd still lounged there against the door, dominating the room without even fully entering it. She'd had that same thought yet again: that he was far too dangerous a game to play. And yet she hadn't moved.

"You deflect and redirect," he'd said softly, as if he'd been summarizing her. Studying her. "You do it every time the topic strays anywhere near something that might require you to express a want, a desire. You're careful only to react, never to act." His brown eyes had seemed, once again, to tear into her. To burn her from the inside out. "Why?" he'd asked in that same quiet way, much worse than the seething anger she'd sensed in him that first night in that same place.

She shouldn't have felt that surge of panic—less in response to what he'd said than to her own suicidal urge to confide in him. She'd been appalled anew at her own capacity for self-delusion.

"You tell me," she'd said. She'd shrugged, as if deeply bored. "I thought I was trying to trap you into being my brand-new fiancé. Is this not the best way to do that? Are you not beguiled?"

"Of course," he'd said, his voice moving

through her like a blow, contemptuous and cold. She'd managed not to react to it, somehow. "Whitney Media and your fortune. How could I forget it for a moment?"

Something hard had seemed to wrap around her then, and Larissa had had to fight off a new, darker suspicion. Why was he so interested in Whitney Media? Why did he keep bringing it up? Was he just like all the rest, even Theo— who would do anything to get their hands on her shares? Not that it mattered, she'd told herself, though something inside her had spasmed around a sharp pain. She'd certainly grown used to that, hadn't she?

"If you want me to leave, Jack," she'd drawled, "you can just say so. You don't have to conduct a highly unnecessary psychological excavation of my inner demons." She'd shuddered theatrically. "That would be a full-time job, let me assure you. And this is your vacation home, after all."

His gaze had darkened and narrowed still further, but he'd only watched her for a long, uncomfortable moment. Larissa had had to fight to remain calm, to appear unruffled, when her body had reacted to his intense, focused attention as if it had been positive. Sexual.

She had despaired of herself. Again.

"What if I want you to stay?" he'd asked, that brown gaze far too knowing, and she'd had to fight the swell of relief—and something else, something far more frightening and far more threatening that she'd refused to acknowledge—that had threatened to take her knees out from beneath her.

"It's hard to believe you're the same man who handcuffed me to his bed," she'd said when she could trust herself to speak. "I'd expect a little more command and mastery in situations like these, and a little less of the leading questions and melodramatic character sketches. You either want me to stay or you don't."

"Nothing with you is ever so cut-and-dried, Larissa," he'd said, straightening from the door. She shouldn't have felt that simple movement as if it was electric—as if it had lit up the whole room. And her. Always her, from the inside out.

"Whereas your behavior is transparent?" she'd asked, ignoring her physical reaction to him—pretending it hadn't been happening. She'd laughed derisively. "Please, Jack. You're about as transparent as a swamp."

"I want you to pack up your things, get in the car and get your pretty little ass back to my house and into my bed," he'd said in a deliberate, too-even voice that hit her like a punch of blistering heat.

His eyes had been dark again with that same all-consuming passion that nothing seemed to extinguish. She'd wondered helplessly if anything ever could. He'd moved closer, until his chest was just a whisper away from her, and her breath had caught. She hadn't been sure if she'd cared what he'd wanted—what he'd been after. And he'd known it. She'd seen it.

He smirked then, daring her. Again. "Is that transparent enough for you?"

Whether or not it had been transparent, Larissa thought now—curled up on one of the absurdly comfortable sofas in the Scatteree Pines sitting room with a butter-soft, emerald-green throw tucked around her to ward off the evening chill— it had certainly been effective. She lost track of days when she was with him—when she was lost in him. And she was, quite obviously, completely lost. She had left the inn several days before, at his command, and had hardly thought about what staying here, in this house, meant for her. What it was likely to do to her. Would she lose track of herself, too? Or was it already too late?

She was afraid she already knew the answer to that. She just didn't want to know it. Didn't want to admit it. It was as if his touch had done more than teach her things she hadn't known about her body's desires, her own capacity for feeling. It had taught her how to let herself hope, too. That terrified her most of all.

She could hear him out in the hallway, his voice

clipped if unfailingly polite, and knew he was talking to his perpetually disapproving grandfather. She recognized the tone of voice he used. She was known to employ a similar one, though she was historically far less courteous, when speaking to her own father.

The thought of Bradford was unwelcome and chilling. Larissa pulled the throw closer around her body, trying to ward off the effect of him from all these hundreds of miles away, as if his very name called down the pitiless beacon of his condemnation, like a laser from on high. He'd left his usual collection of tri-weekly messages on her voice mail over the past two weeks, none of which she'd been able to force herself to listen to. What would be the point? She could recite her own flaws and sins by rote—she didn't need to listen to her cold, vicious father launch into his favorite litany of the same. Nor did she need to hear more examples of his palpable disapproval and active dislike of her to make her feel small. She could do that all on her own, thank you.

She already spent far too much time thinking about the people she'd hurt with her own self-destructive behavior. Just as she'd spent the past days thinking about how she didn't seem to feel that restless need here. With Jack. That she could simply…be herself. Bradford was unlikely to help with that fragile, shimmering new feeling.

She knew enough to remain silent when Jack walked into the room. He threw her an inscrutable glance, but did not stop near the couch where she'd curled herself up into a ball. He moved to stand near the fire, picking up the heavy iron poker and using it against the burning logs with more force than was strictly necessary. She didn't know why that made her long to go to him, to wrap her arms around him and rest her face against his back. As if that might comfort him. As if she was the sort of person who was capable of comforting anyone, much less someone like Jack Sutton.

As if he would let her.

What ideas she was giving herself, the longer she stayed here! She couldn't see any of this ending any way but badly. Horribly. And yet, even knowing that, she didn't move. She couldn't. *Not yet,* she told herself, ignoring the yawning pit in the depths of her stomach that warned her of what was to come. *Not just yet...*

Because she'd had a taste of hope—a glimpse of something she hadn't known she could want, something better than she'd dared imagine—and she couldn't bear to give it up. She couldn't bear to give *him* up.

She was already lost irrevocably, she knew then, with a certain fatalistic sense of the inevitability of it. Perhaps she had been the moment she'd seen him, and she knew she had been the moment his lips had touched hers. She was like a princess in reverse, she thought with a flash of black humor— lost at first kiss, rather than found.

Larissa let her gaze travel down the length of his strong back, marveling anew at the physical perfection he wore so easily, so carelessly, the sweep of clean, athletic lines along with the low-slung jeans he wore like a second skin on this island, where the usual designer wardrobe he was celebrated for in New York City would have seemed fussy, out of place. Here he was as much a part of the land, the great house, as the great pines that towered all around them. He was all lean, smoothly muscled power, danger and desire wrapped in one delicious package. No wonder she could hardly bear to ask herself what his motivations might be. She didn't want to know. She wanted to stay here, out of time and place, forever.

"I hope you gave your grandfather my respects," she said, looking back down at her magazine when he turned toward her, careful to veil any emotion she might inadvertently show him. She risked another glance when she was sure she'd controlled it. "I haven't seen him in years."

Something unpleasant flashed in his eyes then. His mouth twisted, and she felt the bottom of her stomach fall away.

"Is that your endgame, Larissa?" he asked sharply, his voice like a lash. "Is this some extended, desperate attempt to get your hooks into my grandfather? I suppose I should have seen that coming."

She felt as if he'd slapped her, and hard. She had to call on all her years of burying her reactions, her emotions, to contain herself. To keep from breathing heavily—from registering the body blow. It was so unlike her to forget herself so completely, to leave herself so wide open. To forget all the things he'd accused her of doing, of planning, of wanting. Had she really thought *he'd* forgotten all that? His bone-deep mistrust of her, his sneering belief in her ulterior motives? Just because of their sexual chemistry?

She remembered it now. In stark detail.

"I am to marry," Jack said then, abrupt and cold. "Soon. My grandfather has selected a handful of suitable candidates, and he expects me to pick one of them to do honor to our family name. None of them are you. So I suppose he's the next logical choice, isn't he?"

Larissa thought her heart might tear itself into pieces. For long moments, she couldn't move. Much less breathe.

He had called her a whore, and then she had slept with him. Repeatedly. What did that make her? Why was she surprised that he thought exactly that? She'd practically ensured that he would think nothing else, so carried away was she with these intense *feelings;* she'd lost her mind completely. Her stomach knotted hard, then twisted ruthlessly, and for a beat of her heart, then the next, she thought she might be sick. But somehow, she managed to swallow it down, lock it away. Somehow she kept the angry, appalled tears from spilling out and shaming her even further.

If this was what it was like to *feel,* she thought bitterly, she'd been much better off keeping herself completely and totally numb. For years.

And still she raised her brows at him, and forced herself to lounge back against the sofa's cushions, as if she was the very personification of *languid.* As if she was some kind of ancient, reclining empress. She told herself she was furious with him, but she knew better. Jack thought exactly what she'd wanted him—and the entire rest of the world—to think. She'd gone out of her way to make sure they all believed in the Larissa Whitney myth. Hell, she'd believed in it herself for far too long, hadn't she? And with good reason. It was no one's fault but her own that everyone— absolutely everyone, from paparazzo to random person on the street to her own father to this man right in front of her—believed what she'd wanted them to believe.

That she enjoyed that out-of-control, dripping-with-excess life she was famous for. That she was exactly as shallow, greedy, lazy and disappointing as she'd acted. That she never wanted anything from her life but a long, extended party, forever and ever without end. She'd made that bed, no one else. Now she had to lie in it. Over and over again.

It wasn't Jack she was furious with—it was herself.

"Is your grandfather single?" she asked, as if mildly intrigued by the idea—instead of deeply appalled by it and by the fact Jack could suggest such a thing at all. Charles Talbot Endicott was eighty-five years old if he was a day. What did Jack think of her? But she knew what he thought. She forced herself to shrug airily. "I've always liked older men. And I certainly wouldn't have to worry that he was after me for my money, would I?" She aimed her smile at him, mysterious and sharp, burying her feelings beneath it as she always did. As she always would. "I think I'd be an excellent May to his December, don't you?"

The look he sent her then was brutal, but she preferred it to the other part of him she'd thought she'd seen—the part that made her want to cuddle with him as if they were both other people, safer and less complicated people, and thereby opened her up to sucker punches like the one he'd just landed. The one that still had her head spinning.

He likes to have sex with you, she told herself coldly. Harshly. *He doesn't like you. No one likes you. Don't forget that again.*

"Let me hasten to assure you that my grandfather would not touch the likes of you with a ten-foot pole," Jack told her, almost scoffing, though there was something much darker in him. She could feel it even if she could not quite see it. It occurred to her that Jack was just as good at hiding as she'd learned to be. She shook the thought aside.

"By that I assume you mean the likes of me are *pretty,*" she murmured, indulgently, as if she was incapable of feeling his insults. As if they bounced right off of her bright plastic surface. Maybe if she pretended to be bulletproof, she would finally feel that way. Maybe. "And you might be surprised who finds their way to a ten-foot pole when I'm at the other end of it."

Jack shook his head, letting out one of those hollow laughs that usually meant she was getting to the person laughing like that. That she was in the act of disappointing them in some profound way. She congratulated herself on yet another successful round of selling her own myth to the world. Maybe it was time to accept that it would define her no matter what, no matter what epiphanies she reached on her own or how much she knew she'd changed inside. Somehow, right at this moment, with this man, of all men, looking at her as if she was despicable down into her very bones, she couldn't face that with any measure of equanimity.

Not for the first time in her life, she wished she could just disappear.

"My grandfather has been seized with an unusual—and highly suspicious—desire to deepen the family bonds this holiday season," Jack said matter-of-factly, surprising her. But she held herself still, waiting for the next blow. It was coming as surely as the next day's sun. She had no doubt. "We haven't celebrated Thanksgiving together since before my mother got sick. But this year, apparently, my grandfather wants to change all that."

"Will there be a convenient photo opportunity?" Larissa asked. She lifted a shoulder and then dropped it when he frowned at her, as if astounded anew by her shallowness. "That's how we express our familial bond, such as it is, in the Whitney family. We fake it for the cameras."

Jack's gaze seemed to penetrate even harder and further than usual, but then he shook his head. "My grandfather prefers to keep any family gatherings private," he said with a shrug. "The better to vent his spleen without tarnishing the Endicott legacy."

"Surely he can't have anything to vent at you about." Larissa wondered why it was starting to grate on her, this endless pretense that she cared about nothing, no one, not even herself and especially not him. But she kept on, as if she could not feel the chill in the room, or hear the bite in his voice. "You're a paragon of virtue. A veritable saint of our times, dedicated to your acts of philanthropy and other mind-numbingly good deeds. What can he have to complain about?"

Jack fixed himself a drink with tense, controlled movements, and then threw himself on the sofa opposite hers, stretching his long legs out in the space between them. His eyes glittered, and the look in them made her want to squirm.

Larissa wanted to go to him, to reach out to him, but she knew better than to move. He would never accept her as anything but a sexual conquest. A thoughtless, careless whore. One whom he might be able to talk to now and then, given the similarities of their upbringing and stations in life—but only, she thought with a sudden flash of unwelcome insight, because he didn't think she mattered enough to bother dissembling in front of her. Not like the worthy, decent heiresses that were no doubt lined up for him back in Manhattan, all good enough to marry. She wanted to wilt, or possibly die, but instead she raised her chin as if to ward off a blow. She'd do better to keep all of this in mind, wouldn't she?

Jack took a long pull from his crystal tumbler, then stared at the drink in his hand for a moment before turning that icy, assessing glare back on her.

"My grandfather loathed my father from the moment he met him," he said, just as Larissa had begun to think he wouldn't speak after all, that he planned to simply freeze her to death with that frigid stare. "He begged my mother not to marry him. Pleaded with her. But she was young and foolish, and from what I understand, my father was so good at it back then."

"Good at what?" Larissa asked softly, afraid that her voice would break what seemed like a fragile, momentary peace—that he would stop talking to her like this and return to decimating her with all his consummate skill. She preferred the dangerous pretense of this intimacy, she decided, to the bitter reality of his opinion of her.

"At pretending he had depth," Jack said, his mouth twisting. "At pretending he was something other than a complete waste of space. But he was handsome and charming. My mother said he seemed to light up rooms when he walked into them. How could she resist?" He laughed, but it was not a pleasant sound. "She didn't realize until later that that was only his great ego. If he was not a Sutton, and did not have so much wealth and privilege at his disposal—none of which he earned, of course—he would have been known as what he really is." His eyes met hers. "A con man."

When Larissa did not react, when she only looked back at him, forcing herself not to move a single muscle lest he assume she had not gotten his clear inference that she was like his obviously much-despised father, he blinked. He dropped his gaze then, scowling at the drink in his hand.

"As far as my grandfather is concerned, I was fruit of the poisoned tree from the moment of my birth." A mocking sort of smile, ripe with self-knowledge, carved itself into his lean jaw. "And I spent the first thirty-odd years of my life proving him right. I did my father proud. I was, if possible, *more* useless than he had ever been. More full of myself. More of a degenerate. I wasted everything that was handed to me as if that was my job. I was such a prize."

"Why are you telling me this?" she asked—carefully, because she was certain she would not much care for any of his reasons.

His dark eyes met hers. Held. His gaze was stormy, cold and gave no quarter. She felt it like his hands on her body. Like the slap of the words he'd thrown at her earlier, without any warning.

"Because I want you to be clear about what's going on here," he said, his words like bullets, inflicting as much damage. "My mother was the only one who ever believed in me, for absolutely no good reason, and she died before I could prove to her that she wasn't as much of a fool to believe that as she was to marry my father in the first place. My grandfather has never forgiven me for any of it." He leaned forward, his dark eyes intent on hers, bright with condemnation and a kind of fury. "For being born to such a father, for being such a vast and public disappointment to them both. For breaking my mother's heart, again and again, with my antics. My marriage—to a woman from a good family, of good character—is the only possible way I can begin to redeem myself in his eyes."

He said it so simply. Almost easily, as if he agreed with every word. Perhaps, she thought, he did.

"I don't know what you want me to say," she said quietly.

"You are everything the old man detests, Larissa," he assured her, an icy kind of satisfaction gleaming in his eyes, a terrible kind of triumph, as if he couldn't decide whether he liked saying these things or hated them. Or both. "A trial to your parents, a stain on your family's name. Famous for terrible and depraved behavior. Always the talk of the town in the worst possible way. You are his nightmare."

Luckily, Larissa knew all the words to this particular song. Somehow, she told herself, that should make it hurt less. That stabbing pain was unconnected, surely.

"A useless, worthless waste of the Whitney legacy, which I fail to treat with the appropriate measure of reverence and gratitude," Larissa chimed in. "A trial to my long-suffering father. Too exposed, too bold, too unapologetic. Tacky, amoral, stupid, loose." Her face felt stiff, but she forced another smile, this one even deeper. "It's as though you know me."

"I *was* you," he bit out. "Don't you understand? There's nothing you could ever do to shock me. I've already done it all myself." His smile then was derisive, though something moved in his eyes and made her chest feel tight and hollow, all at once.

"I don't think I'm getting the subtle subtext, Jack," she made herself drawl, as if entirely unaffected by any of this. She felt light-headed. Her eyes hurt from the effort of holding back tears she would rather die than shed in front of him. She smirked. "Am I to understand that you will not, in fact, be proposing to me after all? Dirty, despicable me? And here I was, preparing my hope chest."

"You'll never trick me, either," he continued, his eyes too dark, as if he knew just what was in her head. She had to fight off a shiver. "I don't know what you're after here, but you won't get it. I know better than to believe a single word you say and my grandfather would never let you darken the Endicott name. Never. You're wasting your time here, which is your business—but you're also wasting mine."

"What a lovely picture you've painted," Larissa said after a moment. Her voice sounded thin to her ears, too close to weak. But she had been through worse than this, she reminded herself, and she'd survived. What was a little more pain? She should have known better than to give in to something she wanted this badly. When had that ever worked out for her?

"It's the simple truth," he threw back at her. "What I can't understand is why, when you're as intelligent and aware as you clearly are, no matter the lengths you go to try to hide it, you would *want* to live the way you do. It doesn't make any sense."

But Larissa knew there were a lot of truths, and none of them were simple. Anger, misery and her old companion, shame, mixed in her gut. She wanted to scream. She wanted to shake him— to force him to *see* her the way she'd started to see herself. But that wasn't a truth he was ready to face. And she realized that this was better, no matter how much it hurt. It would be far worse to show him the truth about herself, and have him reject it. Her. The *real* her. This way she kept the secret truth hidden, no matter what. And she would make sure that was safe, if nothing else. It was all she had.

"You've foiled all my grand plans," she said when the silence stretched too thin, making sure she sounded bored. She ran her fingers through her hair, carelessly ruffling the short black strands. She rolled her eyes. "Whatever will I do now?"

"Do you think this is a joke, Larissa?" he shot at her, his voice hard. "You shouldn't be here. I should never have succumbed to what I know is nothing more than a regrettable physical weakness. I know what you are, and still I brought you here." His lips pressed together.

"I am a disgrace," Larissa said, her voice quiet even as her eyes met his, and held. She drew the throw from her body, and set it to the side as she sat up. "A cautionary tale to young heiresses everywhere. I'm the boogeyman, aren't I? The emblem of everyone else's bad behavior. They look at me and don't have to feel so badly about themselves any longer. I'm the lowest of the low. People hit rock bottom and it comforts them that they can still look down to see me."

"Stop it," he said gruffly, as if the words were torn from him. As if what she said hurt him, too. "That's not helping."

"It's the simple truth, Jack," she said, throwing his words back at him. "And here are a few more truths. You hate yourself for wanting me. You hate how good we are together, how much chemistry we have. You've hated me for years because I made you face things about yourself you never wanted to see."

She saw the struggle on his face then, the battle. He wanted to fight with her—whether to contradict her or to twist the knife in that much deeper, she didn't know. She only knew that more than that, he simply wanted her. The way she'd always wanted him. Disastrously. Self-destructively. Overwhelmingly and unreasonably. She could see it written plainly across his face—just as she could see how much he wanted to fight it. She wished the wanting itself could change something. She wished it could matter more than all the rest.

"What's your point?" he asked, his voice strained. Maybe this really did hurt him, too. Maybe pigs flew even now in great, lazy loops around Endicott Island. She was an idiot.

"You asked me to come here," she reminded him, the crack of temper in her voice aimed more at herself than at him. But it worked either way. She stood up then, and brushed her hands over her stomach and down to her hips, ostensibly straightening her royal-blue sweater, though she knew the movement also made the material cling to her curves. She was not above playing dirty, after all. "I'm happy to leave. The last thing I need to do is sit here and help you wallow in your own self-pity."

He stood up, too, and they were standing too

close together, suddenly. She didn't know if she wanted to hit him or kiss him. She didn't know which one would tear her further apart. She wasn't sure which one she could survive. Most of all, she didn't know how to feel about the fact that even now, even knowing exactly how low his opinion of her continued to be, knowing that on some level he hated himself for wanting her anyway, her breath still quickened at the thought of kissing him again. Her breasts felt too full, her nipples pulled tight. Her core softened, readying itself for his possession.

She betrayed herself. Again.

He looked at her as if doing so tortured him. He reached over and traced the shape of her cheekbone with his thumb, holding her jaw in his warm palm. The gentleness of the gesture—the implied tenderness—was almost more than she could bear.

"Damn you, Larissa," he said softly. Gruffly. "But I still don't want you to go."

CHAPTER EIGHT

HE WAS losing it.

Jack didn't need another lacerating conversation with his grandfather to point that out to him. He was sprawled out in front of the fire with Larissa's soft, delectable body on top of his, and he was still buried deep inside her. He should have thrown her out earlier as he had half intended to do, but, instead, the only place he'd thrown her had been to the floor—where she'd gone all too willingly, as unable to fight the shattering passion between them as he was. Now she had her face buried in his neck, and he could feel each shuddering breath she drew as she slowly came back down to earth.

He should not have felt so...peaceful.

He stroked her back as a besotted lover might, memorizing the delicate ridge of her backbone, the silken smoothness of her soft skin, the feminine swell of her hips and the sweetness of her firm bottom beneath his hands. He wanted her again, already. Always. Like a randy teenaged boy in the throes of his first crush. She called to him in ways he was still attempting to deny, even to himself—but there was no denying the fact that he couldn't keep his hands off her. He couldn't even stay away from her when he knew, beyond the shadow of a doubt, that she was no good for him.

She was addictive, and like all drugs, she would only destroy anyone foolish enough to fall under her spell. Jack knew it. He'd already kicked this habit once before.

She stirred against him then, making a soft noise into the crook of his neck that made him clench against a need he didn't fully understand, and didn't choose to investigate. She raised her head, and for a moment their eyes met. Hers were that always surprising, so unusual green, golden with passion and reflecting the glow of the fire. She was mesmerizing, no matter what else she was. Deadly, he thought, in the way of the sea all around them that crashed relentlessly into the rocky island shore again and again, with no thought to the consequences.

Her teeth worried her lower lip for a moment, and then she pulled herself up and off him, pulling her knees up beneath her and reaching for one of the throws that had ended up twisted around them. She pulled it around her like a shawl, with her free hand raking back that short glossy black hair that should not have made her look so ethereal.

He studied her in the flickering light of the fire, trying to see beneath the surface. Trying to understand how they had ended up here, when he had meant only to call her bluff all those nights back. It was getting harder and harder to remind himself of the ugly truth of her, when all he could see before him was her exquisite beauty, rendered in black and gold and rose tonight, as if she were a rich oil painting stretched lush and inviting across a canvas in some sunny gallery somewhere.

He winced at his sudden poetic turn. Was this what she did to him? He shuddered to think what might be next. A sonnet? A ballad? But still, he couldn't look away from her. Her elegant neck, her delicate cheekbones, the lush perfection of her lips. He had wanted her for years. Since that damned weekend when he had tasted her for the first time, and he'd never managed to entirely rid himself of this need for *more*. He'd begun to wonder, with no little concern, if he ever would.

"You're staring at me," she pointed out, her voice smoky and low. She didn't look at him. She kept her gaze trained on the fire, though he saw the way her jaw firmed, the way her chin rose slightly, as if she was bracing herself. "Are you waiting for me to transform into the monster you

think I am? Or do you just see that anyway, re-
gardless of what I do?"

Something moved through him then, unwieldy
and raw, and he didn't know how he was supposed
to handle this. Any of this. It was as if he short-
circuited when this woman was around. He lost
all his famous charm, all his purpose and direction. *Himself.* He could see nothing but Larissa.
Every angle of her face, every plane and curve of
her lithe body—he found it all equally fascinating.

She was narcotic. And would be the ruin of
him, if he allowed it. There was no pretending
otherwise.

"You're not a monster," he said, shaking off
the disquieting line of thought. He sat up then,
and moved to prop himself up against the nearest
couch. Unconcerned with his nudity, he merely
watched her, and told himself that the heat in her
cheeks was from the fire. Nothing more.

"What am I, then?" she asked softly. He heard
that odd, almost wistful note in her voice and felt
his eyes narrow as something in him responded
to that tone. As he was no doubt expected to do,
he told himself. She was nothing if not calculat-
ing. Why was that so hard to recall? Unbidden,
he remembered all the things she'd claimed on
that first night. All the lies she'd thrown at him.

"You tell me," he said, because why not play
along with her? Why not see how far she was will-

ing to go? Hadn't that been the point of all of this in the first place? "Didn't you claim you were on a mission to reinvent yourself?"

Her eyes cut to his, a sharp slash of brilliant green, but after a moment she only smiled. "I did," she said, her voice too soft. He could not quite bring himself to believe it. "I did say that."

"So tell me." He didn't understand his own sudden sense of urgency. He didn't understand what he wanted from her. Why draw this out? Why make it about more than the physical? That he couldn't comprehend at all. "Tell me all about your secret metamorphosis."

He was certain she heard the bite in his voice, but she didn't react to it. She only turned back to the fire, that damned smile of hers still clinging to her lips. He hated that smile. He wanted to see the real thing. He knew it was in there somewhere, buried deep in her usual bag of tricks, mixed in with her many illusions and sleights of hand. She was so good at using all her many smoke screens, telling all her lies. He'd seen a shadow of her real smile once, he reminded himself. Just once. He wanted to see it again.

He wanted. That was the problem—he wanted too much. He always had, with this woman. Why did he want so badly to pretty this up into something it was not?

"I was in a coma, not in rehab," she said, surprising him. Her shoulders tensed, but then dropped, and he had the sense that she'd ordered herself to relax. He wished, fervently, that he did not find that endearing. He did not ask himself if he believed her. "And all I wanted when I woke up was for everything to get back to normal—to act as though nothing had happened, because I was so scared. So terrified that everything had changed, that I had changed, and I had no idea how to deal with that." She shook her head. "I hated that everyone *knew*. What had happened to me, that I was so fragile. That I'd collapsed so publicly. I hated it."

He was surprised by the fierce tone she used, and the scowl she directed at the fire, though he understood she was seeing something else entirely. He wondered what. He wondered what her ghosts looked like, what haunted her. What demons she thought lurked within her, if she thought such things at all. If anything she said was true. And then he wondered why it mattered to him. She was the only woman he had ever felt inspired to protect, and she was the one who needed his protection least. It was insanity.

"Larissa…" He didn't know what he meant to say. He hadn't meant to speak in the first place.

"I didn't care that Theo left," she said, ignoring him. She made a hollow sound. "Doesn't that say it all? A person—a real person, a good one—

should care that her fiancé never loved her, not really. But then, a real person would never have gotten engaged to someone that she didn't love herself, so I suppose it doesn't really matter." She shifted, and pulled the blanket tighter around her thin frame. "Either way, he left."

"You don't have to talk about this," he said. In fact, he wished she wouldn't. It was easier when she was playing her usual role, vamping and flirting and acting up in all the ways he expected of her. This was something else altogether, something unsettling and much too close to the kind of realness he'd thought he wanted. But he wasn't sure how he felt about it now that it was happening.

"And…everything was normal," she continued. "Just as I wanted it." She sighed. "But *I* wasn't normal. There was nothing about me that was how it had been before. I should have died, but I lived." She turned to look at him then, and the look in her eyes made something punch through his gut. *"Why?"*

The question hung in the air for a moment. Jack couldn't tear his gaze away from hers.

"Are you asking me?" His voice seemed too loud. Too brash. "Or was that rhetorical?"

Larissa smiled, and while it was not that fake smile he'd come to hate, it was heartbreaking all the same.

"I had no one to ask at all," she said simply. It made something flash through him, sharp and cold. Fierce. "Not my father, who, as you pointed out, has hated me for years. Not my mother, who has lived out her life since I was nine wholly medicated. Not my friends, such as they are. They cared the least. They laughed about my 'wild night' and wanted only to hit the next party and forget it had ever happened."

Jack knew exactly who her friends were. He knew all their games, their obsessions, their addictions and their delusions. Many of them had once been his old friends, his partners in crime. He knew everything there was to know about the circles she ran in. Nothing she was saying should have surprised him. It didn't. Nor did it surprise him that the truth of her condition had been kept quiet—that was how families like theirs operated. But still, there was that vulnerable cast to her face, and it tugged at him. Made him want to wade in and rescue her.

But from what? a cynical voice asked inside his head. *Her own mess? The one she made all by herself? The one she's here to get you to fix?*

"They're idiots," he said harshly. Dismissively. "They always have been."

"It took me almost three weeks to realize that no one was ever going to care that I'd almost died," she said in that same quiet manner, as if the things she spoke of were far too terrible to embellish in any way. He wanted to gather her close, hold her, soothe her somehow. But he didn't know how to reach for her, and he wasn't at all certain she would let him, even if he did. "And another week to understand that if I stayed there, I'd stop caring, too. Which I decided meant I might as well have died as I was supposed to." She faced him then, her eyebrows high, her gaze direct. "People look at me and see what they expect to see. Nothing more and nothing less. So I decided that the solution was not to be seen."

"That's what this camouflage is, then," he said, indicating her hair. She ran her palm over it, smoothing the gleaming black cap against her skull. He pictured the other version of her—all that long, blond hair. The masses of it, the public's obsession with it. The earnest copycats, the snide impersonators. The way it had always marked her, set her apart, made her shine. No wonder it had been the first thing to go, he thought, surprised to feel even that much sympathy for her.

"I decided to see who I was when I wasn't Larissa Whitney," she said, letting her shoulders rise and fall. "When I wasn't in Manhattan. When I wasn't a walking, talking embarrassment to my family's legacy. When I was just me."

What was absurd, Jack thought, was how much he wanted to believe her. How much he already did. When he knew—*he knew*—that she was nothing more than a slick little liar. As good at what she did as his father was. *He* was on to wife number five, who had to be some ten years Jack's junior. Jack knew better than to believe another smooth-talker. Especially one who looked like Larissa, and could turn him so easily to putty in her pretty little hands.

"And how has this experiment worked out for you?" he asked, watching the wariness creep back into her gaze as she heard his tone.

"It was working fine," she said evenly. "Until you showed up."

He actually laughed then. "This is crap," he said. She stiffened, paled, but he ignored it. "You can play make-believe all you want. You can dye your hair every color in the rainbow. That doesn't change anything."

"Of course not," she said, her eyes hard. "Because I'm a monster."

"No," he retorted. "Because you're Larissa Whitney. Your father sounds unpleasant. So is mine. What does it matter? There are bigger things at stake here than interpersonal relationships. Or hurt feelings. For God's sake, Larissa. You complain that you're treated like a *monster*—"

"I've never complained," she snapped out, and there was an affronted look in her eyes then, as if it was crucially important to her that he see that.

"Not directly," he conceded. He shook his head. "But then you turn around and act like a spoiled child, throwing a six-month tantrum because you don't like the situation you found yourself in when you woke up. A situation you made yourself."

"I've never denied that." Her lips thinned. "This isn't a pity party, Jack. I know who I am. I know what I did. I have no illusions about myself at all."

"I'm sure that's what you tell yourself." He raked his fingers through his hair, fighting the desire to put them on her curves instead. But that would only complicate this particular conversation. He blew out a breath. "You might even believe it."

"I'm sorry to disappoint you," she said, but there was a dark undercurrent to her dry tone. She shrugged, and he got the distinct impression that it was a defensive gesture, that it hid something vulnerable beneath. Why did he want to see it—see *her*—more than he could remember wanting anything else? "But I don't think you know me the way you seem to think you do."

"I know that you could have the capacity to do tremendous good in the world, like everyone else who was born to the kind of privileges we were," Jack said, searching her face, wishing he could see behind that damned mask of hers. Wishing he didn't have this crazy urge to *reach* her somehow, to change her. As if anyone ever changed. Much less on demand. Much less a woman like this, crafted of greed and selfishness, a monument to entitlement. "You have an unimaginable amount of money at your disposal and you could have that kind of power, too, if you stopped hiding from it."

"You have no idea what you're talking about," she bit out, but he saw a darkness in her eyes then, and he thought perhaps he'd struck a nerve.

"No one has a better idea than I do," he countered. "Have you forgotten who you're talking to? Whitney Media is your birthright. Pretending otherwise because you have issues with your family doesn't make you strong, it makes you a coward."

"Let me guess," she said, with a bitter laugh. "You want my shares, too, like everyone else."

He met her gaze. Held it. "The only thing I want less than Whitney Media, Larissa," he said, astounded at the depths of his own cruelty, his capacity to hurt her, to *want* to hurt her as much as he wanted to protect her, yet couldn't, "is you."

She looked at him for a long, tense moment. He could see her chest rise and fall, too rapidly, and her green eyes were far too troubled. But when she spoke, her voice was smooth. Relentlessly, impossibly smooth. For the first time, he wondered what it cost her.

"Hilariously," she said, as if she was choosing her words with great care, as if she was afraid they might bite back, "I keep thinking that you've said the worst possible thing you could say—that your opinion of me could not possibly sink any lower. And I am always proved wrong."

"I'm not trying to insult you." He didn't know what he was trying to do. He could only see those beautiful eyes, that siren's face, and he wanted things that could never be. That he could not fully admit. That, if he were smart, he would never permit himself to want in the first place. "But what you do is run away, isn't it? You've never faced anything in your life. You drown yourself in whatever might let you escape from the things you don't like or can't handle. Do you want to know who you really are, Larissa? Just look at what you do."

Her head was bowed by the time he finished, her mouth a tight, flat line, but though her gaze was overbright when she looked up, no tears fell.

"Thank you," she said, and he hated how much he liked the fact that her voice was uneven. That he'd finally gotten to her. That there was something there beneath the mask, the fantasy, after all. That the carefully constructed and maintained Larissa Whitney surface was not the sum of her. She cleared her throat. "And I'm sure that this intervention was launched purely out of an altruistic concern for my character, and has nothing at all to do with the fact that one of the things I ran from—notably—was you."

She could pack a punch. He could admit it. He sat there for a moment, filled with reluctant admiration. He'd never thought to give her any credit for how tough she must have had to be to survive like this as long as she had. For always managing to keep playing this game while showing only the tiniest of cracks in her armor. She was a master at it.

But he had nothing left to lose.

"Yes," he said, holding her gaze, willing her to be what he knew she could not. Wanting it anyway. "You left me that weekend. My mother had just died and I was foolish enough to believe that what happened between us meant something." He smiled coolly. "But don't worry, Larissa. I stopped believing in you a long time ago."

The worst part was that she'd stayed with him after that, Larissa thought much later that night, when he slept beside her in the great iron bed while she lay awake. Much too awake. She stared at the shifting darkness beyond the big bay windows and wondered how she'd let all of this happen. How she'd lost herself so completely, when she had only so recently felt as if she'd recovered some pieces of who she ought to be at all. Or why, after all the things he had said to her and all the ways he had demonstrated how little he thought of her, she hadn't simply left. The sad truth was that she hadn't even tried.

Maybe she didn't believe in herself, either.

Instead, she had channeled all that hurt and fury and pain into the only thing they seemed to agree on—passion. The simple truth of his skin against hers, his mouth fused to hers, their bodies moving together, as one. As if that could save her. As if that meant something more than sex.

And now he slept peacefully at her side, his big body sprawled over the bed in a show of masculine abandon, while her stomach churned and her heart pounded. She could not seem to avoid the truth of things as she'd been trying to do ever since he'd walked back into her life. She'd hidden in the powerful sensuality of their connection, the wildfire of his touch, but she couldn't do it anymore. Tonight had changed something inside her—flipped a switch—and she couldn't pretend anymore. She couldn't let herself go numb and act as if it didn't matter. And she couldn't lie to herself—no matter how hard she'd tried to do exactly that in the past couple of weeks.

Jack hated her.

Her breath left her then, in a jagged rush, even as a kind of tidal wave of anguish crashed over her, raking across her skin and leaving her panting in its aftermath. She turned to her side and curled into a ball, hugging herself tight. It was true. He hated her—he had for years. Oh, he might like the chemistry between them. He couldn't keep his hands off her! But in every way that mattered, on every level beyond the physical, he thought she was worthless. He did not need to actually sneer at her—his every word and action did it for him. A sneer would be superfluous.

And maybe that wouldn't have felt quite so terrible to her, quite so shattering, if her own feelings weren't just as painfully obvious to her in the cold and the dark. What she felt for Jack Sutton defied all reason and logic. It was too big, too chaotic. It *hurt.* She must have suspected that feeling so much could be damaging, she thought, or why would she have gone to such lengths to avoid it for most of her life? She'd stopped visiting Provence when she was a girl because she'd thought it had hurt too much to leave. She hadn't known she could feel so much that she wondered if it was some kind of heart attack, as if it was something she might not survive intact. Or at all. If this was what *feeling* was like, some part of her thought she'd been better off when she'd been incapable of it.

She wanted him in ways she had never imagined one person could want another. In ways she had never known she could want anything or anyone.

She hurt. For him.

She didn't simply want to lose herself in the wild glory of their physical connection, though there was part of her that wanted only that, even now—she wanted him to *know* her. To *see* her. To understand all the things she'd never dared say out loud, and would never risk saying to him. She, who had spent the whole of her life making sure that no one could ever peek behind that curtain. She, who wasn't even sure what there was to see back there, where no one had ever gone, not even, she knew, herself.

But every time she looked at Jack, it was harder and harder to keep up her act. It cost more. It seemed to leave deeper marks. And the truth was, she was so tired of it all. Exhausted. Of herself, of her image, of the fact those things were held to be interchangeable. She had never felt the need to defend herself before—and how could she when she was guilty of everything they accused her of, and no doubt more besides—but knowing that Jack believed the worst of her made a hollow space carve itself out in the center of her chest. And it yawned wider and deeper the longer she spent with him and the more he looked at her as if she was only confirming his lowest expectations with every word she said, every expression that crossed her face.

Which was what she'd wanted, after all. What she'd set out to do the moment she'd laid eyes on him. Because that was what she did, that was how she survived—she showed people whatever they wanted to see. She was whoever they wanted her to be. So why should it bother her so much now? Why should she feel as if it was killing her—actually, physically killing her—to let him think the worst of her?

But she knew why. The impossible, unwanted truth clawed at her insides and made her clench her hands into fists, panic and terror and a ferocious kind of joy she'd never imagined before storming through her body—but she knew.

There were words for the way she felt, but she could not bring herself to use them. Not those words. Not for her. She was Larissa Whitney. She had set her course long ago, and she knew with a certain grim matter-of-factness that the things others took for granted—those happily-ever-afters, those white picket fences—were not on the table for her. Not ever. Even the most docile and well-behaved members of her social circle could, at best, look forward only to the sorts of lives their parents had laid out for them at birth. Impersonal marriages, necessary children to carry on the family lines and inherit the family wealth, eventual affairs and hushed-up scandals, and the slow, inevitable slide into high-functioning substance abuse that was ruthlessly suppressed at the great charity balls at which all of Manhattan society appeared to lie so eloquently to each other about their supposed happiness.

That was the kind of dutiful marriage Jack would have, she knew. To some fresh-faced, in-offensive girl who would never know the way he could tear her apart in bed. But that bright prospect was not for Larissa, not unless she was very, very lucky. She was too notorious. And if her life had taught her anything—if Jack had taught her anything—it was that she was certainly not likely to turn up *lucky* anytime soon.

Larissa sat up, swinging her legs over the side of the bed and clenching her toes against the cold floorboards at her feet. She couldn't help looking back over her shoulder at Jack, fighting back the spike of heat behind her eyes, the echoing tightness in her chest, her throat. Outside, the clouds shifted and the moon shone in through the tall windows, only highlighting his heartbreaking perfection. He was all the things that she'd never admitted she wanted. He was still so golden, so impossibly beautiful. He wasn't tainted, as she was. Ruined beyond repair. He wasn't scandalous, the punch line to jokes, everybody's favorite warning.

She could have him, she knew, if she could just find a way to overlook the way he felt about her. If she could simply close her eyes and tolerate it. If she could pretend it didn't matter, that it didn't hurt. If she could resign herself to living as the creature he saw when he looked at her instead of who she really was—whoever that might be.

It scared her that she was tempted. So terribly, seductively tempted. There was far too much of her that wanted to just climb back in the bed, curl up into his heat, and let him treat her any way he liked. Anything, if she could stay with him a little bit longer. Anything, if she could just hold on to him for a while.

But she couldn't do it. Because she might not believe in herself either, but the difference was that she knew she should. And she wanted to.

For long moments she sat there, paralyzed. Panicked. But she knew what she had to do, however little she wanted to do it. This time, he did not reach for her. This time, there was no confusion. He stayed fast asleep. She had to decide on her own, with no interference.

And so, eventually, though it took more courage than it should have and far more than she'd imagined she possessed, she stood. She couldn't let herself look at him. Her mind played out scenes for her instead. Jack's cool brown eyes, searing into hers. His flashes of tenderness, here and there, over these past long days. His careful, gentle hands juxtaposed with his wicked, delicious mouth. His cruelty. His kindness.

How could she leave him? *Again?*

She remembered that long-ago weekend then, with a thud of recognition in the vicinity of her heart. She might not have had the clarity she did now, but even then, she'd known that Jack Sutton posed a much greater threat to her than all the other issues in her life combined. She could not even have said why. She'd only known that she'd had to go, though her body had longed for him and the intensity of it had dizzied her. She'd sneaked out of his apartment while he'd been in the shower, as if she'd had something to be guilty about, and she'd jumped on the first plane to Europe. Then to the Maldives. By the time she'd returned some weeks later, Jack had stopped looking for her. She had told herself, repeatedly, that it was just what she'd wanted. And then she had told herself that she might as well accept Theo's latest proposal. She had told herself it didn't matter anyway, that she had simply gotten carried away that weekend with Jack…but on some level she'd always known the truth.

He was too much. He was too dangerous. He was the only man she could ever imagine falling in love with, she was terrified that she already had, and she could never, ever have him. Not really. Not the way she knew she'd end up wanting him, with all of her heart and her soul. She'd known that then, and it had made her panic.

She knew it now, and it was worse—because

she'd glimpsed what things could be like between them. All the things she'd never known. This house, filled with life and family, so much so that it clung to the very walls. This private sanctuary of an island, where there were no cameras, no expectations. The two of them, alone here, being exactly who they were instead of who they were supposed to be. She'd allowed herself the fantasy, the *what if.* That little slice of hope. If her life were not so complicated. If he were not so determined to be above reproach in his grandfather's particularly Puritan way, and marry appropriately—do his duty. If she could be someone else, someone he could be proud of, or at any rate not ashamed of.

If he did not think she was, in fact, some kind of whore.

Her chest hurt when she pulled in a breath, and when she let it out it was more like a sob. She stifled it with her hands. This time, she was not numb. Not at all. This time, she knew exactly what she was giving up. And she couldn't believe how deep the hurt of it went, how it made her legs feel hollow and her stomach twist into knots. Part of her would have done anything, put up with anything, pretended anything at all, to make that go away.

But Jack had inadvertently taught her—simply by existing, by causing this very riot of feelings in her—that she deserved more. Not because he offered anything like it, she thought bitterly, or thought *the likes of her* deserved it, but because she was no longer willing to settle for less. Eight months ago she wouldn't have cared if she was with someone who hated her, but she wasn't that person any longer. She might not know who she was, really, but for the first time since she'd woken up from her coma, she had an inkling of who she wanted to be. And she didn't hate herself. Not anymore. So how could she stay with someone who did? It would mean going back to that numb, paralyzed place, and she couldn't do it. Not again. Not knowingly.

She dressed quickly and quietly in the pale light of the November moon, then piled her few things haphazardly into the small bag she'd been living out of these past months. She let herself look at him one last time, held her breath to keep from sobbing, and ached. Oh, how she ached. For everything they would never be, and for all the things she knew he would think of her when he woke to find her gone.

But it was better this way.

It had to be.

There was a ferry leaving at dawn, just as he'd told her in the beginning, and she would be on it.

CHAPTER NINE

JACK was deeply bored. Possibly terminally bored.

The Metropolitan Museum of Art was splendid, as ever—and he knew all about its many charms in exhaustive detail, having had several ancestors involved in its founding. Jack had spent so much time in the famous and much-beloved landmark that he was fairly certain that he could blindfold himself, wander away from the tuxedos and lavish gowns that dotted the Charles Engelhard Court in the American Wing for tonight's charity event, which was indistinguishable from all other charity events as far as he could tell, and find his way by memory alone to the Medieval Sculpture Hall where, he knew because it was December and thus tradition, he would find an eighteenth-century Neapolitan Nativity scene and the famous candlelit tree.

The fact that he had any such urge at all, despite his long-held dislike of all holidays and any decorations thereof, only confirmed what he had already suspected the moment he'd picked up his date for this predictably ostentatious evening to benefit the good cause *du jour:* he was not going to marry Miss Elizabeth Shipley Young despite his grandfather's fervent desire that he do so. Not when he could not imagine how he was going to get through the night without expiring of acute disinterest right there in the center of the grand party, tucked up at a banquet table lavishly decorated with holly and mistletoe, with his grandfather on one side and the entirely too beige and uninteresting Elizabeth on the other.

"Are you all right?" his date asked, her voice trilling as she laughed—no doubt nervously, Jack told himself, and why not? He had been nothing but grim and humorless since the moment he'd arrived at her apartment building earlier in the evening. Restless, preoccupied. Able only to mouth the expected pleasantries. Not quite the debonair Jack Sutton she'd been expecting, he was sure. No charm, no grace. It was as if he'd left that part of himself back on Endicott Island, awash in all the rain.

But he knew she wouldn't see all that. They never did. She would see *Jack Endicott Sutton* no matter how he behaved.

"I couldn't be better," he lied, forcing a smile. It felt stiff. Strained.

He did not have to look to his left to know that

his grandfather was sitting there, with perfect posture and a beetled brow, watching Jack's every move as if the force of his will would lead to the wedding he wanted that very evening. But the smile dropped from Jack's face the moment his date excused herself to find the ladies' room, and despite the fact he was surrounded on all sides by the gossipy piranhas who made up New York's highest society and his own deeply censorious relative, he couldn't seem to force it back into place.

"You're about as charming as a pallbearer tonight," came the inevitable gruff voice from beside him. Jack checked his impatience. Barely.

"I'm here, aren't I?" He raised his brows at the old man, daring him to comment further. "As commanded."

"I shouldn't have to *command* you to do your duty to this family," his grandfather began, his august forehead crumpling into a scowl as he began the familiar complaint. But Jack was too out of sorts tonight, too irritable. He couldn't take it the way he usually did.

"You don't *have* to worry over my dedication to my duty at all," Jack said from between his teeth, his tone still technically polite, still respectful, if only barely. "You *choose* to. I have long presumed it is one of the great joys of your life."

His grandfather eyed him for a long, tense moment, and Jack braced himself for the inevitable storm. He wondered idly when he'd become so reckless—when he'd stopped walking around on the eggshells he'd always felt littered the ground between his grandfather and himself. But his grandfather only sniffed before turning away and engaging the person on his other side in conversation.

Jack lounged back in his chair and stared up at the looming old bank facade that dominated the far wall of the great courtyard. But he hardly saw it. He admitted the fact that he had not quite been himself for several weeks now, however little he wanted to admit anything of the sort. And he knew why. He had been this way since he had woken up to find that Larissa Whitney had run away from him.

Again.

He just couldn't seem to get past that.

He'd carried on, of course, as if he hadn't cared one way or the other. He'd told himself that he hadn't. He'd closed up the house and headed for the mainland. He'd suffered through the indignity of a long, drawn-out Thanksgiving dinner at his grandfather's old townhome in Boston's elite Louisburg Square, as ordered. But while he'd calmly assured the old man that he had every intention of settling down and carrying on the family name as expected, while studiously ignoring his father and his father's latest wife, he'd been unable to think of anything but Larissa.

His grandfather had listed the pros and cons of every supposedly appropriate heiress under the age of forty on the East Coast, but Jack had only seen one pair of stormy green eyes, one decadent mouth and that sharp intelligence she went to such great lengths to hide. His grandfather had pontificated about the merging of great families and the responsibilities visited upon those with legacies to protect and nurture throughout the march of time—and he had thought only of her defiance in the Scatteree Pines sitting room, half-naked like a goddess and far more powerful, far more compelling. How, he had wondered while picking dispiritedly as course after course of traditional plates were laid in front of him, was he ever going to settle for someone *appropriate* when he could still taste Larissa? Still feel her? Still *want* her with every cell in his body?

Not that he had mentioned that to his grandfather.

It was as if he'd been enchanted, bewitched. As if he still was. Jack could think of no other explanation. She was just as addictive as he'd feared, and he was just as susceptible as he'd always been. Why had he thought he could control that? Her? And he wanted her. God help him, even now, weeks after and in the midst of Manhattan's finest, even though she'd left without so much as a word, he still wanted her. He could think of nothing else, like a man obsessed.

If he was honest with himself, he thought darkly as he rose to pull out his date's chair with all due chivalry and seat her once again at their table, he didn't particularly care to think of anything else. He had come back to New York and back to his daily work overseeing the Endicott Foundation and all that entailed, but all he thought about was her. He even dreamed about her.

She was his own personal ghost, and he was well and truly haunted.

So he was not particularly surprised, when he heard a low murmur run through the crowd, to turn and see Larissa herself striding into the gala, as if he'd conjured her into being with his *wanting* alone. He felt her presence jolt through him, electric and low, and for the first time that night—in weeks—his smile was not forced at all. Though it felt hard, fierce and entirely focused on her. Much like the rest of him.

She was stunning, but then, he should have expected that. She was not an icon of her generation by accident, and he should have remembered that the Larissa he'd seen in Maine was the unusual version. Hadn't he thought it was a fake? An attempt to manipulate him? And yet it still took a moment for him to reconcile the image of her he had in his head—heartbreaking face scrubbed clean of cosmetics, faded jeans, his old sweaters—with the incomparable beauty that stood before the assembled throng, smiling her Mona Lisa smile for the photographers as if she had never been more at ease, more delighted to be out in public and once more the focus of all of Manhattan's salacious attention.

And she had it, as Jack expected she'd known she would.

"Larissa Whitney has nerve, all right," Elizabeth Shipley Young murmured, in that snippy way that indicated that was no compliment. She let out a catty little giggle that set Jack's teeth on edge. "You'd never know the truth about her from the way she walks around, would you? Like butter wouldn't melt in her mouth."

Jack eyed his date for a long moment, fighting the urge to reach over and throttle her. He doubted his grandfather would approve. And besides, he was supposedly a gentleman. He tried to remind himself of that.

"I didn't realize you knew Larissa," he said finally. Icily. Elizabeth flushed at his tone, or perhaps it was the way he was looking at her.

"I don't," she said, edging away from him in her chair, as if he had slapped her. "Not personally."

"Then perhaps you don't know the truth about her at all," Jack said with barely contained ferocity, the kind that Larissa had routinely laughed at. This woman cringed. "And should therefore think twice before discussing matters that make you look like little more than a small-minded gossip."

Elizabeth gasped, and turned a bright shade of red. Jack could feel his grandfather's hard glare on him, but he couldn't seem to bring himself to care too much about that—or about the date *and* the wedding plans he had just ruined. He was too busy trying to understand why he'd reacted that way to Elizabeth's comment. Hadn't he said far worse about Larissa *to* Larissa herself? Why should it bother him so much when someone else concurred?

His eyes found her again as she moved through the crowd, smiling as if she had every expectation of being bathed in adulation, as if she had descended from some great light to grace this party with her presence. She was poured into a spectacular midnight-blue dress that defied gravity, clinging as it did to her perfectly lithe form and making it clear to all that she required no undergarments. Its many glittering beads sparkled in the lights from above, making her seem to glow and shimmer with every breath, every movement. God, she was even more beautiful than he'd remembered. Jack found that he loved the way she'd made herself up, the better to emphasize those unusual eyes and the shocking glory of that short black hair, somehow styled tonight to make her look far more elegant and sophisticated than her old blond locks would have. She exuded mystery, sensuality, and something else—something new.

And then it clicked. It was her pedigree. Her heritage. All those centuries of the Whitney legacy that she'd never really seemed to accept as her own before, funneled into a certain bedrock confidence. *You might whisper about me,* her very walk seemed to say, *but you will recognize me.*

She was who she was. There was only the one of her, and no matter how notorious she might be, she was still a *Whitney.* Seeing it in this woman—*his woman,* that insane part of his brain insisted—made his body hum with that same, familiar electric charge.

Larissa Whitney had come home.

And Jack couldn't wait to get his hands on her.

Much later, he caught up to her on the iconic steps outside the Museum, high above Fifth Avenue. She was wrapped up against the bitter December cold, but he was still overheated from the long evening spent watching her as she danced with whoever asked her, smiled prettily for whoever approached her, and acted the perfect little heiress, a credit to her family at long last.

He didn't believe it for a moment. He told himself that disbelief was what fueled him, what made anticipation flood his veins.

"Slow down, Cinderella," he said when he was close enough to reach out and touch her—but somehow he restrained himself at the last moment. If he touched any part of her, he knew, he would touch all of her. Here, now, the frigid weather be damned.

She whirled around, and he had the very great pleasure of seeing the Larissa *he* knew peek out from behind this exotic creature with the perfect Society mask. He could see her in the eyes, the faint tremble of her courtesan's mouth, before she ruthlessly hid it away.

"Jack," she said, in a flat sort of greeting. She produced a smile, but he believed it cost her, and he liked the idea of that more than he should have. "Do you make it a habit to sneak up on women walking alone in the night in large cities?"

"Where are you going?" He sounded dangerous. He *felt* dangerous, as though something prowled in him and might leap out at any moment and run wild down the city streets. Or simply pounce on her and devour her. He shifted, feeling edgy and restless. He watched her swallow—watched the elegant line of her throat and he wanted to put his mouth there, against the soft sweet skin—

"I didn't realize my itinerary was your business," she said, her voice nearly as icy as the air around them. Her eyes were cool too, her face that perfect mask, that *presentation* that he hated nearly as much as her ubiquitous smile, which she aimed at him now. "Do you really want to be seen talking to me? On the steps of the Met for all of Manhattan to see? You don't want to risk contagion, surely."

Her voice was sweet, her gaze sharp. He felt each like the slap it was, when his last memory of her was of her head thrown back, crying out her pleasure as she sat astride him and rode them both over the edge. Then she'd fallen against his chest, still making those small, sweet moans, the very recollection of which made him harden. He shoved the memories aside. They were unhelpful, to say the least.

"Here you are, running away from a gala after you went to so much trouble to convince everyone there that you'd left your old ways behind you," he said, his gaze trained on hers, on that pretty mask she wore. "What a surprise. Is there anything you *won't* run away from?"

But she was different from the woman he'd thought he'd known, however shallowly, in Maine. He saw no particular expression in her gaze, no reaction there at all. She only smirked, and he hated it.

"It seems that my interest in unsolicited character assassinations has dimmed somewhat since

I last saw you," she said, her voice like a blade. The smile she showed him then cut as deep. "It's delightful to see you again, of course, especially when you are not pretending to be one of the locals in your fisherman's costume but are back to your usual splendor." She waved a dismissive hand at him, over the exquisitely cut coat that hid the beautiful tuxedo beneath. "But I have somewhere to be."

"What's his name?" Jack meant his voice to be soft, easy, and yet somehow he felt as if the menace in it echoed out into the depths of Central Park and rebounded off the avenues. Larissa went very still. He saw the pulse pound in her throat. But she did not look away.

"Do you mean my date?" she asked. Her tone became scathing. "I came alone, Jack. Grown women can do that, you know. All by themselves. Even me."

"I mean the man you're running off to meet," Jack said, and his tone was nothing short of lethal, though she did not seem to notice. "The man you crawled out of my bed for."

She let out a soundless breath, betrayed by the cold air that turned it into a cloud. Jack smiled. Not nicely. He hardly knew himself, and yet he could not seem to stop.

"Was it that idiot who danced with you four times tonight?" he asked, picturing the dissipated, mean-eyed creature who, he'd felt, had held her far too tightly for far too long. "He looks like a fine choice. I believe he mistook my grandfather for a waiter."

"Chip Van Housen?" Her voice was dry. "Hardly." She made a scoffing sound, as if the very idea were insulting.

"Then who?"

She studied him for a moment, that beautiful mouth flattening. "Because there must, of course, be a man," she said, as if she was coming to a conclusion for both of them, and not a pleasant one. "Given my proclivities. Or is it my profession? I can't keep it straight." She threw up a hand when he moved to speak. "Damn you, Jack," she hissed at him. And then her eyes slammed into his, hard and green. "It's none of your business either way."

Horns complained down in the street. Buses squealed to a stop at the lights along Fifth Avenue, and all around them Manhattan sparkled with light and energy, thousands of lives rushing past them at top speed. And all he could see were her sea-green eyes and the faintest hint of trembling in her lower lip, almost indiscernible. Almost. All he wanted to do was sweep her into his arms and carry her off, and he wasn't even sure if he wanted to throw her onto his bed or, far more dangerous and confusing, simply hold her for a while. Apologize—for always seeming to hurt her, when that wasn't at all what he wanted.

But he didn't know how to say that—and he refused to think about what it might mean. He just concentrated on the woman who haunted him even now, even when she was standing right in front of him.

"Do you really believe that, Larissa?" He moved closer, fiercely glad that she wore those absurdly high heels that let her look him right in the eye, and let him get that much closer to her gorgeous mouth. Close enough to inhale that intoxicating kick of vanilla and *her*. His hands twitched with the urge to touch her. "Do you really think it's over just because you walk away? Again? Do you think it's going to be that easy this time?"

"What do you want, Jack?" She wasn't playing any longer. He could see it—could see the woman he recognized again in her stormy green eyes, so much like the sea. He could hear it in her voice. He could feel it in his chest.

"I don't know." His own voice felt as if it was torn from him, as if he could no more control it than he could her.

"Do you really want to know about Chip Van Housen, of all people?" she asked, her voice hoarse with an emotion he couldn't name. "I used to enjoy him because being with him hurt Theo. That meant I got to do something to Theo *and* indulge my self-destructive streak—two birds with one stone." Her mouth twisted and her eyes flashed. "He thinks I owe him something, but then, he's nothing but an overprivileged bully. He thinks the world owes him something, too."

"And you don't?" He eased even closer to her, then indulged himself—and an urge he couldn't quite explain—by reaching over and brushing one of the slightly longer strands of her hair away from the sweet slope of her forehead. He did not imagine the way she shuddered. He did not fantasize the way her lips parted.

Just as he did not imagine the perfect silk of her skin, or how it felt beneath his fingers.

"What do *you* think I owe you, or the world, or anything else?" she asked, a hitch in her voice. "What price do *you* think I ought to pay? Because clearly, you think I have reparations to make. Why don't you tell me what you think they are?"

"That's not what I meant," he began.

"You're not the only person in the world who gets to decide they want a better image," she threw at him, her voice fierce. "It's just that when you do it, you're greeted with a ticker-tape parade. Some of us have to reinvent ourselves in the absence of accolades and fawning sycophants."

"Still with this story of reinvention," he said, shaking his head, furious with her suddenly. Furious and something else, something raw, that moved through him and left only scars behind. "Why do you play these games, Larissa? What do you hope to gain?"

For a moment she looked as if he'd hauled off and slugged her, hard in the belly. He saw her breathe, as if it hurt her to try, and then her mask slid back into place. But he couldn't seem to reconcile that bruised look in her eyes with the master manipulator he kept telling himself that she was. That she had to be, or nothing made sense.

"Your date looks lovely," she said quietly. Viciously—or that was how it felt to him. Like a hard, deliberate slap. "Speaking of things we have to gain. I'm sure she'll make the perfect, dutiful little wife for you, just as your grandfather decrees."

He didn't care for the way she said that, with that light in her eyes.

"Because you think that you, of all people, know who the perfect wife for me might be?" he asked. He dared her. "Based on what, exactly?"

"She looks sufficiently overawed," Larissa bit out. "I doubt she'll even notice when you start having your inevitable affairs, like all the rest of these people do—she'll no doubt be relieved. She doesn't strike me as the adventurous type."

"Not like you," he said, deliberately. He tilted his head slightly to one side, as if studying her. "Are you offering yourself as my first mistress?"

"No," she said. "It won't be me." Some emotion shone in her eyes, terrible and big, but she didn't look away. "I'm sure it will be someone, but it won't ever be me."

"You're a liar," he told her, only aware that he was all but whispering after the words were out. And still that ferocious anger moved through him, and he worried it was not anger at all. "And a coward. Do you really think you can keep running? Do you think that pretending to be respectable will save you?"

"I've had enough—" she began, furiously.

But he couldn't pretend any more. He stopped her the only way he knew. With his mouth. With all the passion and rage and longing he'd been carrying around for weeks.

He kissed her until he forgot everything, and there was only her. Her taste, her scent. The *fit* of her. He held her face between his palms and kissed her again and again, each taste soothing the wild itch inside of him, even as the fire that always flared between them grew hotter. Higher.

He kissed her until he forgot everything. Where they were, who they were. Who they were supposed to be tonight, here. Who could be watching.

He only wanted to be inside her. Above her, below her, beside her, just so long as he was so deep within her he couldn't tell where he ended and she began. God, what he would give to be inside her again!

But she made a small noise in the back of her throat, and, impossibly, she pulled away.

"Larissa…"

"You don't want me, Jack," she said, her voice ragged. "You want what you think I am. What you see when you look at me. But you don't want *me*."

"You don't know what I want," he threw at her. And he worried that he didn't, either.

"I don't care what you want," she retorted, her eyes dark. And he knew, with a kind of lurching sensation, as if the world had just been bumped—hard—that this was the real Larissa. This, right here. Just as he'd always wanted. But dark and angry and in pain. "I care what *I* want, and it's not this. Kissing a man who hates me, in secret, in the dark, while the girl he might marry sits waiting for him somewhere brightly lit and *appropriate*."

"I do want you," he argued, trying to move closer, but she stepped away, and the way she looked at him seemed to tear into him. Like knives.

"You don't know me at all," she said dismissively. "You want a fantasy. They all do. It has nothing to do with me and it never will."

"I know you better than you think I do," he said, his heart pounding at his chest, his hands aching from not touching her, not holding her, not changing her mind the only way he knew how.

"No," she said matter-of-factly. "You don't. But I know you." Her green eyes seemed to glow then, lasering into him. "You feel perfectly comfortable tearing me to shreds for my every perceived flaw when all *you* do is dance to your grandfather's tune. You can never do enough penance, can you, Jack? And yet you can never bring your mother back, or make your grandfather treat you better."

"Shut up." It was a cold order, as cold as he suddenly felt, as if the December night had taken over his soul.

"You would rather live the rest of your life in misery than stand up to one old man," she said, as if she was unaware of the danger. "You would even marry at his command, as if this was 1882, and yet you go to such pains to tell me how *I* am the nightmare in this scenario. I'm the weak one, the embarrassment. Of the two of us, at least *I* don't pretend to be anything but what I am." Her chin rose. "Flaws and all."

"Says the woman who has made her whole life a monument to shirking her own birthright!" Jack threw back at her, unable to process the riot of emotion inside of him. The shock, the fury. And something else he couldn't quite identify. Recognition? But she couldn't be right about him, could she?

"You don't even see me, Jack," she said sadly. "You never will."

Her eyes seared into him, and he knew, somehow, that he had lost her. Failed her. That she might be the one leaving—again—but he was the one who had made this happen. He couldn't quite grasp it. Her mouth trembled, but she stepped away, and he knew she wasn't coming back to him. Not tonight. Perhaps not ever.

"Larissa..." he said, but it was too late. She had already turned, and was making her way down the steps toward the street.

Leaving Jack to stand there, alone, trying to figure out what the hell had just happened and what he planned to do about it.

CHAPTER TEN

LARISSA waited for her father in the same chilly salon in the Whitney mansion where she had spent many an unpleasant moment in her youth. The room was tucked away on the second level, toward the back of the grand house that sprawled over a whole Manhattan city block and still inspired passing tourists to stop and take photographs of its famous facade. This particular salon was Bradford's favorite. It was small enough and unused enough to allow Bradford to give voice to the full breadth and width of his eternal displeasure without fear of being overheard by the staff.

If she closed her eyes, she was sure she would be able to see herself at all ages, sitting in the exact same position on the exact same uncomfortable chair, staring at the exact same Mary Cassatt painting that had always hung on the wall, casting a false impression of familial harmony over the small, tastefully blue-and-pale-yellow room. But she did not close her eyes; she was much too afraid that she would see Jack if she did, and she had already spent too long this morning tending to the damage a long, sleepless night during which he had taken over her head had done. She blew out a breath, her lips tingling anew at the memory of that kiss outside the Met last night. His beautiful face, his mesmerizing chocolate eyes…

The December light shone crisp and cold through the windows, making Larissa wish she had not surrendered her winter coat and warm scarf to the butler when she'd arrived. The door snapped open then and her father strode inside, dropping the temperature another twenty degrees with his forbidding expression. Bradford Whitney looked as he always did: gray with displeasure despite his exquisite yet understated wardrobe and the great care she knew he took with his skin. Even tyrants could be vain, she reminded herself.

"I am not fooled by this latest display, Larissa," Bradford said, his form of a greeting.

He sniffed disdainfully as his gaze raked over her. Larissa did not let herself react. He sank into the chair opposite hers, across the fussy little coffee table that had sat in that precise spot since the 1800s. They had both assumed their traditional positions, Larissa thought, checking a sigh. Bradford would now unleash his usual bile and Larissa would attempt to survive it intact. There had been years when she'd wept. Screamed. Stared out the window and pretended he wasn't there. Acted as if she were asleep. Made sure she was as comfortably numb as possible. None of it mattered. The entire charade made Larissa feel arthritic, gnarled and knotted with a kind of grief for the life they'd never had, the father and daughter they had never been, and the sort of family the Whitneys could never become.

"I don't know what you mean," she said, though she did. She wanted him to say it out loud, as if she thought the echo of his own ugliness might shame him. It never did. That was yet one more example of her own perversity at play, she thought—something she'd been indulging far too much of late. But she shoved thoughts of Jack aside. She was already battered enough, thank you. Just being back in this house, this monument to her family's long history of delicately gilded and extensively funded dysfunction, made her feel raw. Bruised. There were too many ghosts, too many *could have beens,* crowded in the elegant rooms, stalking the hushed, grand halls.

"I mean all your suspiciously demure charity event attendances of late," Bradford said, a sneer in his voice though he was too well-bred to *actually* sneer at her. This early in the conversation, anyway. "Your sad little gestures toward decent behavior, for all of New York to comment on. Your new wardrobe, as if anyone can forget your outrageous attempts to be shocking in the past. A few weeks of playing dress-up hardly erases a lifetime of embarrassing behavior."

Larissa ran her hand along her perfectly tailored charcoal trousers, and resisted the urge to tug at her fitted black cashmere turtleneck, or to adjust her tasteful diamond earrings. She knew she looked chic, if conservative, and that her impractically heeled boots gave the outfit a little bit of punch. He could not possibly see the shame, the humiliation, that coiled inside of her, that he'd helped put there. He saw only what she showed him. So she showed him absolutely nothing.

"I assume that's your version of 'welcome home,' Dad," she said dryly. Almost serenely. "Thank you."

"The doorman at your apartment building informed me you reappeared several weeks ago," Bradford snapped, as if he hadn't heard her. It occurred to Larissa that, quite possibly, he never had. "I then had to track your escapades through the society pages, waiting for the other shoe to drop, as it always does. Whatever you think you're doing, Larissa, it is having the usual effect. I am not amused."

"I'm fine, thank you," Larissa replied lightly, as if he'd asked. As if it would ever occur to him to ask. "The months away—especially after such a terrible ordeal—really helped me figure a few things out. I appreciate your asking after me. The abundance of paternal concern is touching."

"I'd advise you to be careful, Larissa." He spat out her name as if it was a curse.

"Or what?" Her tone wasn't even challenging. Why bother? She knew that he viewed her very presence as the challenge. She raised her brows at him, more inquiry than attack. "Could my reputation or circumstances be any worse? I think you've run out of effective threats."

"I'm not interested in another scene in your never-ending melodrama," he said, his voice cold. Bored. And quiet, as it always was when he was being the most cruel. "The next time you try to kill yourself in one of those clubs, or at one of your parties, make sure to complete the task. The clean-up is expensive, tedious and reflects poorly on this family and on Whitney Media." His gaze cut into her, arrowing directly into that throbbing core of shame—of hurt, of desperate self-loathing—that she still carried around with her no matter how much she might have otherwise changed. "And I cannot afford to lose another CEO thanks to your games. Do you understand me? Am I making myself clear?"

She had to sit there for a moment and breathe, just as the doctors had ordered her to do eight months ago, when Bradford had sent her into a panic attack in this very same house while addressing a topic similar to this one, and she'd thought it was heart failure. She refused to give him the satisfaction of seeing her react like that again.

"Perfectly clear," she said. She forced herself to produce that damned smile of hers again, the one that hid everything and that she knew infuriated him. "My next coma will be terminal, I promise." She met his gaze, bold and unafraid, no matter how she felt inside. "Are you happy now?"

"You are the greatest disappointment of my life," Bradford told her, almost conversationally, though his cold eyes never left her face.

"A point you have made sure to hammer into me since I was approximately six years old," Larissa replied. She took pride in the way she managed to sit so casually in the stiff, hard chair, as if she were perfectly relaxed. As if she were bulletproof, finally. "I assure you, I am aware of your feelings, and if I was not, I think your request that I make sure to *really* commit suicide next time would have clued me in. I think we can safely say we're on the same page."

"I hope you enjoyed your little vacation, Larissa." No expression. Nothing at all behind his cold eyes. Had there ever been? She repressed a shiver. "I can't begin to imagine what you got up to for so long, nor do I care. The only saving grace is that you managed, somehow, to keep it out of the papers for once. I assume the bill is astronomical, as ever."

Only emotionally, Larissa thought ruefully, but she only shrugged. Let him think she'd hidden away somewhere at great expense. Let him think whatever he liked—she knew that he would anyway, no matter what she said or did.

"Don't think I'll help you if you've exceeded your quarterly allowance," Bradford continued in the same softly vicious way. "I'm done cleaning up your messes." The first hint of emotion she'd ever seen crossed his face then, and she found herself holding her breath. Was this it? Was this when her father revealed himself as being in possession of human feelings after all this time? "Do you have any idea what it meant to this company to lose Theo Markou Garcia? Because of *you?*"

She should have known better. What was surprising was that she felt anything at all, that she could still hold out hope for this man on any level. What kind of fool did that make her? She breathed out again, and summoned up her usual careless smile.

"You do know, Dad, that you and the company are not the same entity, don't you?" She let the smile deepen. "I really do fear for your sanity sometimes."

"After the stunt you pulled with those shares, you're lucky I don't cut you out entirely." Bradford seethed at her, still with that shocking hint of emotion in his gaze. Larissa should have known that it would only—could only—involve his investment portfolio and his beloved bottom line. And that damned company he loved more than anything else in the world. "Don't think I've forgotten what you tried to do—signing our future away for no other reason than to cause me trouble. The next time you change your will, you'd better hope you really do die, or trust me when I tell you that I'll make you regret you ever lived."

That hung there between them, unmistakably vile in the crisp winter light.

"No need," she said sunnily, as if it did not bother her in the least, as if it were some pleasantry instead of his customary ugliness. She waved a languid hand in the air. "Twenty-seven years of your parenting has accomplished the same feat."

"All you had to do was marry Theo," Bradford said, his voice dripping with contempt. "And you couldn't even manage that, could you? You can't do anything, and you never could. Even he didn't want you in the end—and this after the besotted fool chased you around for years."

Larissa could not help but think that Theo was much better off as far away from the dank hole that was the Whitney family as he could get. As she had always wished she could be—as she had tried to be, for the past eight months. But if Jack had taught her anything, it was that there was no running away from who she truly was. It had a nasty way of turning up in the middle of a fall storm on a nearly deserted island, and forcing her to face it head-on. *Lesson learned,* she thought bitterly.

"I'm not here to talk about ancient history," she said quietly. "I can hardly recall any of it anyway." That was not entirely true, but she couldn't help but enjoy the flash of temper in his cold eyes. "You called me here, remember? Surely you have something other than Theo to discuss." She lounged against the stiff back of her chair. "If not, by all means, keep ranting at me. It makes me feel so warm inside."

Bradford stared at her for a long moment, his small, meticulous mouth thinning to a hard line.

"The annual Board of Directors meeting is next Thursday," he said, as if intoning a pronouncement from on high. "I know your attorneys have been attempting to contact you for weeks. Months." He sniffed. "Your presence, while undesired, is required."

"What a lovely invitation," she murmured. She schooled her expression, keeping it deliberately, ruthlessly impassive. "But why? You know business bores me. Especially yours."

She watched him closely, once again looking for

something—anything—to let her know that there was a real person inside her father. That there was some hope for him. But all she could see was his habitual contempt. It was all she'd ever seen.

Was it any wonder she'd turned out the way she had? A small, revolutionary voice inside her asked then. Wasn't the real surprise that she *hadn't* ended up far worse? Surely the fact that she was pulling herself together at all, that she'd survived, had to count for something. Bradford had never been anything less than a monster.

"You will formally sign over your shares to me," Bradford told her, his stern tone brooking no argument. "I see no reason to continue this proxy nonsense, when it is perfectly clear that you have no interest in ever taking your place on the Board. Thank goodness. The sooner we dispense with the formalities, the sooner you can wash your hands of Whitney Media." His eyes narrowed. "And the sooner I can wash my hands of you."

"Does signing over my shares sever our blood relationship?" Larissa asked mildly. "Next Thursday will be a day of myth and wonder, indeed."

"You will not cause a scene, Larissa," Bradford continued, cold and implacable. "You will sign the papers, make an appropriate statement about your intentions to waste your life as you choose, and then you will leave. I don't care where you go. Is that clear?"

Again she felt the ache inside her, the longing for things that had never been. She wished she were a stronger person. She wished she could fully, wholeheartedly believe that he was the monster, not her. She wished she could simply stop caring what Bradford thought of her, what he'd always thought of her. But he was who he was. Her mistake had long been in assuming there had to be something she could change, or fix, to make him love her. To make him tolerate her. To make him treat her with anything but his contempt.

She knew better now. She was a different person, but he was exactly the same as he'd always been. He was the reason her mother whiled away her days in a haze of opiates in Provence. He was the reason she had spent the whole of her life so desperately committed to her own destruction, wildly hoping that something might force this man to care about her. He would never see the change in her. When he looked at her, he saw only who she'd been, who he'd made. An empty, contemptible vessel to the very core.

She knew better now.

"Don't worry, Dad," she said, careful to keep her voice even. Light. As if this wasn't a goodbye. As if she hadn't changed at all. As if he could. "I understand you perfectly."

* * *

Jack was waiting for her in her building's magnificent art- deco lobby when Larissa hurried inside some nights later, shivering from the relentless chill outside and another night of charity balls and rebuilding bridges. Her eyes found him immediately, as if compelled from across the polished marble expanse. He was tall and imposing in his black coat, his gorgeous face set into a scowl that she had no doubt was meant to make her quail in her high heels. And perhaps even douse the whole sweep of Central Park West and the Upper West Side with the force of his displeasure.

He was a powerful man—there was no denying it. But Larissa told herself that she was immune. That she did not feel her stomach drop. That she could not feel the crackle of the usual flames, lighting her up from inside and making her burn. She smiled at the ever-present, fully liveried doormen who prided themselves on recognizing everyone of note in Manhattan—many of whom resided in the famous two-towered Emery Roth edifice on Central Park West that Larissa had called home for years—who, she was sure, knew exactly who Jack was.

"Why are you here?" she asked as she walked toward him. He leaned up against one of the great pillars, as much a work of art as the precious canvasses that graced the gilt-edged walls. She took care to keep her expression unreadable, but wondered how successful she'd been as he seemed to look right into her. Through her. As if she were made of glass.

He looked at her for a long moment, and her heart stopped. Time screeched to a halt, and she could see nothing at all but that storm in his dark eyes. That simmering passion, that fire. Why did it still call to her? Why couldn't she be as immune as she told herself she wanted to be?

"I don't know," he said. So simple. So devastating.

Larissa came to a stop a few feet away from him, and ordered herself to breathe. To swallow. To function.

"This is coming perilously close to stalking," she managed to say, her throat far too dry. "Though I suppose when one is the great Jack Endicott Sutton, one cannot, by definition, *stalk*. One can only *persist*. Or is it *persuade?* Either way, it involves a lofty pedigree and the nation's goodwill." Her smile was thin. "Lucky me."

"I thought that if I called you, you wouldn't answer," he admitted gruffly, those bittersweet-chocolate eyes trained on her, very nearly making her forget that she had moments before been freezing in the usual shock of December in New York City as the heat of him seemed to engulf her. He was lethal.

"You are very astute, Jack," she said. She attempted to smile, but was not at all sure she managed it. "It's one of the things I admire so much about you."

She came to a stop in front of him. The heels she wore gave her height, and made her feel more powerful. Or, anyway, less likely to crumple to the ground and beg for his love, his touch, she told herself. Close to him, she felt that same pull again. That inevitable compulsion. She wanted to bury herself in his arms. She wanted to taste him again. She wanted him more than she could admit to herself, and it hurt more than she wanted to believe it could.

But she couldn't have him, she reminded herself sharply, ignoring the desperate pounding of her heart. Because she was no longer an empty vessel, self-destructively willing to accept whatever scraps were thrown her way, no matter how much it hurt her, because anything was better than that yawning emptiness.

She had to remind herself—forcefully—that this was a good thing. It was.

It was.

"Invite me up," he said. She could hear the implacable command in his voice, could read the bright gleam of passion in his dark gaze. She knew exactly what he wanted. She could feel the answering thrill of it in her own body, threatening to make her shudder in anticipation. In helpless desire.

"I don't think that would be at all wise," she said after a long moment, unable to break away from the way he was looking at her—from the way that gaze held her, as tightly and as securely as if she was in his arms. She stuffed her hands deep into the pockets of her sleek winter coat to keep from reaching out to him, to keep from compounding the terrible mistake she'd made in Maine.

"When has anything between us been wise?" he asked, his wicked mouth curving.

But change was a full-time thing, Larissa thought, no matter how much she wanted it to be otherwise just then. It wasn't just for the moments in which it *felt* right, or when it was convenient. If she wanted to respect herself, she had to *act* as if she respected herself. Always. Even when she wanted to pretend she didn't care about such things and lose herself with this man she was afraid had ruined her forever.

She could feel him breaking her heart even now.

"I'm sorry," she said as evenly as she could, and turned toward the elevators. "I can't do this, Jack. It's been a long week, I have a Whitney Media Board meeting to survive tomorrow morning, without any fiancé to save me as you seem to think I need, and I'm tired."

"Wait." There was a short, tense pause. "Please."

She pivoted back toward him, caught by that surprising last word, and then by the look on his beautiful face. As if he was as lost as she was. As if this was as overwhelming for him as it was for her. As if.

Wishful thinking, she told herself.

But her treacherous heart beat harder. And worse, *hoped.*

"Walk with me. Have a drink with me." His voice was low. Urgent. If he was another man, she might have called it desperate. "Somewhere relentlessly public." His dangerous mouth crooked slightly, and she felt it. Her toes curled inside her boots. Her stomach tightened against a flood of heat. "What could be safer than that?"

But she knew that *she* was not safe. That she would never be safe around this man, because she would always want what he could not, would not, give her.

And she couldn't do that anymore. She wouldn't.

She stepped closer to him, steeling herself against the rush of longing. She heard his swift intake of breath as she leaned in and pressed a kiss against his lean jaw. She let her eyes close, briefly. She let his clean, male scent tease her, ignite her. And then she forced herself to step back. To move away.

"Goodbye, Jack," she whispered.

His hands moved, streaking across the distance

she'd placed between them, holding her upper arms in his grasp. Not hard. But he wasn't going to let her walk away, either. Not this time.

"How can I see who you are, Larissa?" he asked fiercely, his voice curling around her, through her. His gaze cutting deep. "How can anyone, if you do nothing but run and hide?"

Her eyes felt too big for her face, too bright, and he, meanwhile seemed to take over the whole world, as if nothing had ever existed but him. As if nothing ever would. How could she love this man so much when she knew, with every fiber of her being, that he would be the very thing that destroyed her? That he had already laid the groundwork—that he was nearly halfway there? Or that she was his willing accomplice?

"You could use the eyes in your head instead of your prejudices," she managed to say, fighting to the end, because she knew no other way. "That's a start."

She'd meant to keep her voice light, easy. The way it normally was. But there was nothing normal about the way he looked at her, his eyes too dark, so much tension in his jaw, as if he was fighting the same demons that she was.

"Show me, then," he whispered. "Show me."

And she was still so weak. And she loved him. And the fact that she was sure that both of those things would contribute to her eventual doom did nothing to make her heart stop pounding, or her breath stop coming so quickly. Too quickly.

He was here, and she was in love with him, and she couldn't help wondering why doing what was right seemed to *feel* so wrong. It was one thing to succumb accidentally to a force like Jack. It was something else to choose it, deliberately. To *decide*.

Which she kept doing. Following her stupid heart, instead of her much smarter head.

"Okay," she said, before she could think better of it. Before she could remind herself of all eight million reasons it was a terrible idea.

"Okay?" He echoed her, but his dark eyes were already blazing with a kind of hard, male triumph, and she felt his hands close tightly against her shoulders, almost convulsively.

"You can come up," she said, and there was no pretending that her voice was anything but raw, that she was anything but vulnerable. Somehow, in that moment, she didn't care. Or it didn't matter the way that she knew it should. She met his gaze, held it. "But you can't stay."

CHAPTER ELEVEN

SHE couldn't manage to convince herself that it had been a mistake, Larissa realized the next morning, as she carefully reapplied her lipstick and then eyed herself critically in the mirror of the executive washroom high in the Whitney Media tower that thrust proudly into the sky over midtown Manhattan.

Though it was. Of course it was. How could it be anything but?

Her eyes slid shut involuntarily, as images from the night before chased through her mind, tantalizing her, arousing her all over again. They hadn't made it more than two steps into the apartment before they'd fallen on each other, the weeks apart having whipped them both into some kind of passionate frenzy. It had been a kaleidoscopic blur of mouths meeting, hands exploring, clothes being shoved out of the way—and then, at last, the elemental bliss of his hard thrust into her.

A shiver skated over her skin at the memory,

that same old fire searing through her all over again. Jack was as lethal in her own head as he was when he was directly in front of her. Perhaps more so.

They had not spoken then, awash in ecstasy on the thick Persian rug that graced her foyer. Eventually she had led him back through the sprawling apartment to her bedroom that looked out over Central Park. All the lights of Manhattan had sparkled before them, and she'd felt them all like licks of flame within as he'd stood behind her there and kissed and tasted his way down her neck, her back—divesting her of the remains of the gown she'd been wearing, the shoes. And then he'd turned her around, his hands so sure, so demanding, so hot against her hips, before he'd knelt down before her and licked his way into the hot, molten center of her, sending her spinning off over the edge yet again.

She'd screamed his name, wild and unrestrained as the passion crashed through her, and had been somewhat surprised that she hadn't shattered the wall of glass behind her with the force of it.

She laughed at her own reflection then, the sound very nearly rueful in the privacy of the lush bathroom suite. Why couldn't she banish him from her head? Why did her traitorous body exult in even the memory of him? Why was she so bound and determined to love the things that hurt her the most?

Larissa returned to her inspection of her image in the glass, ordering herself to concentrate. She toyed with her hair, and confirmed that her cosmetics were applied with the appropriate skill to emphasize her seriousness and not her notoriety. Her clothes performed the same task—a narrow, deep brown pencil skirt and a creamy white soft blouse separated by a bold belt, all of it over high-heeled, ankle-strapped shoes. She thought she looked far more *businesswoman* than *attention-seeking socialite.*

But she was all too aware that most people would see only what they expected to see. In fact, she was banking on it.

"Why are you going to the Whitney Media Board meeting?" Jack had asked much later the night before, when they'd lain side by side on the bed, sated. For the moment. Larissa had felt herself tense. "I thought such things bored you," he'd continued, his voice no more than idly curious.

She'd opened her mouth to play it off, to deflect his attention in her usual way, but she'd stopped. The only light in the room had come from outside, fickle and pale. They'd been caught in shadows, together on the bed and yet, she'd thought, ultimately so very far apart. And yet… His voice hadn't been accusing. It hadn't been derisive. It had been…careful.

"I can't say that I know if it will bore me or not," she'd said quietly. "I've never actually attended one before. My father and Theo preferred to pat me on the head and send me on my way, because they liked to handle everything." She'd laughed. "Not that I had any interest in it, of course. I was happy to be free of it."

She had felt Jack's big, lean body sprawled next to hers on the wide bed, had felt the thrust of his attention in the dark room, his keen focus on her, even when she'd closed her eyes. It had been as powerful as his touch, as demanding. She'd wondered what he'd been looking for—what he'd been trying to see. Or did she simply, foolishly, wish that he'd wanted to see beneath the surface? She'd shifted, curling on her side to face him, able to pick out the blurred suggestion of his features in the dark, the glitter of his eyes, the comforting solidity of him, so big and so male. It had been so late in the night that it had *felt* later still. It had felt close, confessional. Intimate. A time outside the rest of their lives.

Or perhaps she'd only wanted to think so.

"My father wants me to sign over all my shares to him," she'd said. She'd let out one of her best laughs. Tinkling and bright. False. It seemed to rebound off the glass window as if off the city itself, and she'd regretted it. "Apparently he thinks that ending my relationship with Whitney Media will be the same as ending his actual relationship to me. Which, given his obsession with the company, is true enough." She'd sighed then, shifting position on the mattress. "He is, of course, delighted at the prospect."

Jack had let out a breath, and Larissa had braced herself, expecting one of his blows. Expecting him to tear her up in the usual way. Would he tell her this was all self-indulgent crap, too? But instead he'd turned so that he'd faced her on the bed, propping himself up on one arm.

"I saw my father at Thanksgiving," he'd said in a low voice. He'd reached over and brushed her hair away from her forehead, almost absently, making Larissa's throat feel tight. "He is, in fact, one of the main reasons I loathe the holidays. I'd managed to forget why, in all these years." He'd shifted. "In between the usual lectures from my grandfather, I got to sit back and watch while my father drank every drop of whiskey in the house, and then proceeded to feel up his practically teenage wife at the dinner table." He'd let out a short sound, too hollow to be a laugh. "To be honest, I don't know that he has any idea that I exist. I doubt he remembers that we have a relationship to sever."

Something had passed between them then,

in the dark. Something full and deep, that had seemed to expand inside Larissa's chest, making her feel at once too big and too small. She'd had to remind herself to breathe. She'd been unable to look away from him. She'd wanted to crawl inside him and stay there until everything that hurt, everything that was complicated, faded away. As if he had the power to make that happen.

"What will you do?" he'd asked, his voice hushed. *Reverent,* she'd thought, and the scariest part was that there'd been no tiny little voice to castigate her for that kind of presumption.

But it had all been too much, and she'd been too afraid, in the end, to take it any further—that fragile communion. She'd been unable to let herself trust it. Not fully. No matter how much, how desperately, she'd wanted simply to fall into him and believe that he could catch her.

That he would want to catch her.

It had frightened her, as had something else, something far edgier—that she'd wanted something like that at all. She, who had walked alone for so long. And yet she'd wanted it. Him. Hadn't she always wanted him, no matter how foolish the urge? She'd wanted all of it more than she'd wanted to admit to herself, much less explore.

But she'd been hurt far too many times by her own desires, hadn't she? There was changing herself for the better, and there was recognizing her own flaws and missteps—and neither one of those things made trusting Jack Sutton anything but a folly of the worst kind.

"Larissa Whitney is not known for her corporate interests," she'd said instead, her voice perhaps too scratchy. Too obviously, dangerously raw. "She is much too flighty, and probably deeply unintelligent, as well. She would be a distraction, nothing more."

"She has an Ivy League education and centuries of power in every cell in her body." Jack had contradicted her in his quiet, sure way, making her limbs feel too hot, too weak. He'd smiled—she'd heard it shape his words in the cocoon of darkness, and his fingers had traced the shape of her jaw, her lips. "I think she can handle it."

That was what she would cling to today, Larissa told herself now, pushing through the heavy, silent door that led back into the hallway. Not what had happened next, that had left them both covered in a fine glow and sound asleep in each other's arms. Not his departure—as she had demanded, she reminded herself, and not for the first time— some time before her alarm went off. *He thinks I can handle it.* It made something happy and warm move through her, no matter how many times she told herself that it didn't matter—that it had been just something he'd said in the middle of the night, that she shouldn't take it to heart.

That it didn't mean he hated her any less.

She walked along the corridor, her heels sinking into the plush carpet. The executive level of the iconic Whitney Media tower boasted phenomenal views of Manhattan out of every window, and the interior was no less impressive. Priceless art graced the walls, paying homage to both the Whitney family legacy and Whitney Media's long history in newspapers, movies and television. Hardwood floors and polished chandeliers shone. Every step whispered of wealth. History. The Whitneys.

Larissa had been here more times than she could count. First, as a child, trotted out on special occasions to pose for the cameras and play the role of cherubic blonde moppet, Bradford's supposedly beloved child. Later, she'd attended functions as a surly teenager, and after that she'd spent far too much time in this building as Theo's date. But this was the first time she'd walked down the deeply carpeted halls by herself, under her own power, as someone whose name was etched into the stone of the building itself instead of just an accessory. She decided she liked it.

She glanced at the slim gold watch on her wrist as she rounded the final corner, and knew that she'd timed this perfectly. She smiled politely at the efficient-looking secretary who sat sentry outside the conference-room doors, and paused, pulling in a deep breath to calm her nerves. To prepare herself. She thought of Jack's hands, tender on her body, cupping her face, almost as if there was affection there. Almost… She thought of his voice, telling her to claim what was hers, whether she wanted it or not. Daring her to try. Daring her to consider herself in an entirely new way, though she wasn't sure she could have admitted that to him.

And that had been before he'd said those things last night.

I can do this, she thought. *I really can handle this.*

And then she pushed the double doors open and sauntered inside.

The room smelled of testosterone—the deeply moneyed Wall Street kind, resplendent in elegant suits, four-thousand-dollar hand-crafted Italian shoes and sheer, bone-deep self-satisfaction. The kind that made and lost other people's fortunes without notice on various stock exchanges, all before their afternoon tee time. Larissa saw in a glance that she was the only woman in the room, and also the youngest person by several decades. That surprised her about as much as the inevitable look of displeasure on her father's face—which was to say, not at all.

"Gentlemen," she said, flashing her famous smile as she moved to the only empty seat and settled herself into it. "I hope I haven't kept you waiting."

There was a murmur of reply, more uninterested than not, but Larissa assumed that was largely by rote. It didn't matter. She knew more than enough about every man in the room, and she found them not nearly as intimidating as a scrum of nasty paparazzi snapping cameras at her the morning after some new debacle. She didn't need these men to be polite, and she didn't much care if they weren't. She didn't need them at all.

"You are five minutes late," Bradford said in his heavy, disapproving way. "But there is no need to draw this out. The papers are ready for your signature."

He thrust a finger toward the ominous stacks of paper set out on the gleaming surface before her. Larissa glanced at one, flipping a page or two, marveling at the convoluted language. Like Bradford, it was all a lot of sound and fury to cover the actual, unpleasant truth within.

"At the moment, I hold the controlling interest in Whitney Media, isn't that right?" she asked idly, still looking at the sheaf of papers in front of her.

There was a humming sort of silence, thick with male shock, and she could all but *feel* the way they looked at each other—all of them far too busy and much too important to deal with the likes of her. All of them affronted at her temerity. She was a disposable object, to be manipulated at will. Wasn't that how Bradford had always treated her? Wasn't that how she'd always behaved?

She was enjoying herself.

"Just sign the papers, Larissa," Bradford snarled at her. "We have actual business to attend to here once this exercise is completed."

"Fifty-one percent, if I'm not mistaken," Larissa drawled, ignoring him. She leaned back in her chair. "Or is it fifty-two? Theo signed his shares over to me before he left. A lovely gift, really, in light of our broken engagement."

"What kind of game is this?" one of the other men demanded, loud and jowly. Larissa knew that he ran a hedge fund or two, owned the better part of lower Manhattan, and was generally held in some awe in the highest investment circles. And she wasn't afraid of him, either. She focused on her father, who was turning a spectacular shade of pink as he glared at her.

"Not one I'm interested in playing," Bradford said, so cold and hard that icicles seemed to form on his words as they hung there in the air between them. Larissa only smiled.

"It's interesting to me that you threw all your time, energy and emotion, such as it is, into this company, yet never thought to make any provisions for its future," she said, still in the relaxed tone she was sure was as much an affront to every officious man in the room as was her refusal to simply sign away her birthright as ordered. Or perhaps as was her very presence. "Not very practical, Dad, is it?"

"The plan for the future was Theo, and you're the one who ran him out of here," Bradford snapped. "Not that I imagine you care in the least. What is this, Larissa? The paparazzi not paying you enough attention lately? You should fall out of a few more limousines. See if that scratches the itch. But stop wasting our time."

"This is hardly a waste of time," Larissa said, still smiling at him. She let her gaze travel around the room then, lighting on each man in turn, challenging each of them. Daring them to contradict her. "This is a board meeting, and I am the majority shareholder. My attorneys tell me that the bylaws of this corporation insist that the majority shareholder sit on the board. And so here I am, at your service."

She calmly ignored the higher volume of the muttering, and watched her father instead, as he fixed his ferociously cold glare on her. If he could have wrapped his hands around her neck, she knew without a shred of doubt, he would have. She found that there was a certain power in knowing that, however sad it was. However little it said about their relationship. But this was not the cold, controlled Bradford she knew. This man was far angrier. This man, she realized, finally had something to lose.

He'd never cared much about his daughter. But Whitney Media was something else entirely. Whitney Media mattered to him. It was the only thing that ever had. She felt a deep jolt of an old sort of pain at that, but thrust it aside. He didn't deserve her longing for might-have-beens. He never would.

"You have voted your shares through a proxy for years," Bradford said, clearly seething as he stared at her. His hands were in fists. If she were a better person, Larissa knew, she would not take such pleasure in that. But she never had been any good, had she? As her father had been the first to tell her. "You can hardly expect anyone to take you seriously now that you've decided, for some perverse reason of your own, to change that."

She let her smile deepen, Mona Lisa to the last, as she leaned back farther in her seat and lounged prettily in the manner she knew infuriated him.

"I don't feel that I need a proxy any longer," she said simply. "But thank you."

"Then there is the small matter of your obnoxious and embarrassing notoriety," he continued, as if she hadn't spoken. His icy glare sharpened, became a weapon—a direct attack. She ordered herself to remain perfectly still—seemingly unaffected. "You are, quite clearly, not fit, Larissa.

Not in any way. Not for anything, and certainly not to sit on this board in any capacity."

He thought he'd won. She could see it. It gleamed there in his eyes.

"Then I suppose it's a tragedy that there is, in fact, no morals clause," she replied coolly. "No commentary on unrelated behavior, whether falling out of limousines or the Gramercy Park Hotel or the front door of the Whitney mansion. Not a single 'too notorious to take her rightful place' entry in the bylaws, I'm afraid." She let her smile sharpen. "Of course, the entire board would be disqualified if there were any of these things, given that notoriety and bad behavior is largely in the eye of the beholder, don't you think?" She shrugged without dropping her gaze from his. "Just think what I could make of yours."

"Sign the goddamned papers." He bit out the words, and it was if the rest of the room disappeared. There was only Bradford. Only the father who had loomed over her whole life, casting his shadow far further than he should have done, and far deeper. But that was her past. This was her future, and she got to decide how it went. Starting here.

"No," she said quietly, powerfully, enjoying this moment perhaps more than she should, but knowing that it was the first step toward a new, better life. A real life, at last. She wished that somehow Jack could have seen her turn into the person he'd suggested she could be in the middle of all that rain on Endicott Island. But that was a bittersweet kind of pain, better left for another time. She let her smile turn to something close to real. "I'm sorry, Dad, but I'm not going to do that."

Another night, another gala.

Jack managed to keep the expression of boredom from his face as he dutifully stood with his grandfather on the splendidly lit and amply heated outdoor terrace of the Museum of the City of New York, high up on Fifth Avenue with all of Central Park spread out before them, dark and inviting, on the other side of the street. Not for esteemed hostess Madeleine Doremus Waldorf any petty concerns about the weather or the season; she was known for her outrageous society events, and this one, held out of doors when the temperature hovered around seventeen degrees, was precisely the sort of thing she adored. There were enough space heaters to make sure that the younger socialites could show off their Pilates-toned arms in their sleeveless sheaths, the older society matrons murmured about Madeleine's "daring," and all Jack could think about was Larissa Whitney.

More specifically, the fact that he knew she was here tonight, and yet he had not seen her at all. More specifically than even that—the fact that it had nearly killed him to leave her the night before last, naked and soft and warm as she slept, and he still did not understand why he'd done it. He could so easily have stayed, despite what she'd said, what he'd tacitly agreed to do. He'd wanted to stay. But he'd found he could not bear to be another man like her father, who ignored what she said to suit himself.

He was in so much trouble.

"Don't see how standing around in the December air like lunatics will raise any money for this charity of hers," his grandfather said in his gruff voice. "It's far more likely that we'll all die of hypothermia first." He muttered something else that sounded a lot like *foolish women,* which Jack diplomatically chose to ignore.

There was a lot of that going around tonight. Jack was ignoring his own highly inconvenient and terrifying feelings for the most inappropriate woman in New York. He'd been ignoring those for quite some time, if he was honest. Possibly for five long years, were he to get technical. He was studiously ignoring the ramifications of *that* line of thought. He was also ignoring the inevitable presence of his father, some thirty feet away, making an ass of himself with his child bride. Jack was taking his cues on that from his grandfather, who had been icily ignoring his son-in-law for well on forty years.

"Happy holidays, Grandfather," Jack murmured, as close to sincere as he could manage under the circumstances, which was, perhaps, not terribly close at all. His grandfather's canny blue eyes, so much like Jack's mother's, swung to meet his, the usual cool assessment in them raking Jack from head to toe.

"I'd be a lot happier if I could die in peace, knowing that the Endicott line will not end with you," he said, his brows drawn together. "But apparently, you would prefer to insult every heiress in Manhattan instead of living up to your responsibilities."

Jack shook his head, feeling his mouth thin. He was weary of this conversation, as ever. But then, out of the corner of his eye, he saw her. She emerged from the great doors that led inside the building, and paused there for a moment, flanked by a veritable phalanx of Manhattan's best-known and most philanthropically inclined young heiresses. Her peers, in other words. They were all engaged in animated conversation, and there was no denying the fact that Larissa looked at perfect ease in their company. There was a time she might deliberately have worn something shocking, something far too outrageous for a staid event like this, but if that Larissa still existed, Jack saw no sign of her tonight.

He let himself stare. This Larissa was radiant. Like a beacon that sent light spinning out from the party and into Fifth Avenue, then on into the dark of Central Park beyond. She seemed to glow in a beautifully fitted gown in a rich magenta hue that clung to her delicate shoulders, wrapped tightly around the delectable perfection of her torso like an embrace, and then flowed to the floor. She wore a magnificent necklace, all sparkle and shine, that seemed to rival the winter stars high above them. There was the demure hint of the same sparkle at her ears and on one wrist, and she held a bright little clutch in one hand.

She made his chest tight and his body hard from all the way across a crowded party.

He was in so much trouble.

This Larissa was claiming her world, Jack thought, with some mixture of pride and panic. And he couldn't help but think that somehow, despite all the tumult of what he did not want to feel and what he could not help but feel, he had already lost her.

"That one," his grandfather said with a disparaging snort, his penetrating glare boring into Larissa. "No, sir. That one has bad news written all over her. She's been nothing but trouble since the day she was born."

"You don't know her, Grandfather," Jack heard himself say, his tone clipped. "You don't know what kind of trouble she was handed. Perhaps a little compassion is in order."

"I know what kind of trouble she makes," the old man retorted, unmoved. "And that's more than enough, and far more than most." He turned to look at Jack again, his blue eyes narrowed. "She's no different than your embarrassment of a father. All the same morals and all the same actions. You'd be well advised to find someone else to be fascinated with, young man."

And something in Jack…snapped.

He felt it like a loud crack, deafening for a moment, and then his hearing cleared. Everything cleared. He'd never felt so focused. He looked at his grandfather, at the old man's trademark scowl and that censorious glare, and then he looked back out to find Larissa, only to discover that Chip Van Housen had cornered her yet again. He could see that her smile was fake across all of these people. All of these useless, unnecessary people who lionized him and demonized her and had never truly seen either one of them. He couldn't stand it.

He couldn't stand any of this.

"Enough," he said.

His voice was not loud, but it had the hard echo of finality, and he saw his grandfather register it with some surprise. He looked at the old man, and felt something ancient and hard crumble to dust inside of him. His guilt, he thought dimly. That abiding ache for the things his mother would never know of him. His sense of regret that he had come from such a father. He'd been carrying these things around for so long now he'd come to think of them as part of him, twisted together into some kind of phantom limb.

"I beg your pardon?" But his grandfather was looking at him closely, and Jack knew he'd heard him perfectly.

"I'm sorry, Grandfather," he said. And he was. But he was also resolute in a way he'd never been before. "I'm sorry that I was not the grandson you hoped for when I was a younger man. I'm sorry that nothing I do can change the way you feel about me. Some part of me looks at my father and cannot even blame you." He thought of Larissa's words outside a different museum, and shook his head. "But I can't pay penance any longer. I don't want to."

"This is about that girl?" His grandfather's voice was incredulous. Appalled. "That trashy Whitney girl? Why would you want to align yourself with that kind of disaster?"

"What I want is my business," Jack said evenly, with a steel edge beneath. "I have catered to you for years out of a sense of loyalty and respect, but you have accorded me none in return. And I am tired of acting the meek, cowed little schoolboy because you feel the need to put me in my place again and again and again." He shook his head. "I've had enough."

"Jack…" his grandfather began, that heavy frown beginning again.

"I'm sorry you hate me," Jack said in a low voice, holding the older man's gaze with his. "I truly am. But I can't let that rule me any longer. I can't change it and I'm tired of trying. I'm the future of the Endicott family legacy, Grandfather, whether you like it or not. You're just going to have to trust me."

His grandfather stared at him for an arrested moment, his blue eyes wide. From beyond them, Jack could hear the band play, the cultured voices swell in the air and his own father's too-intox-icated laughter drift on the night breeze. And he knew that no matter what happened here, he would not regret saying these things, much as it grieved him to hurt the old man even further. It couldn't be helped. This was long overdue.

"I don't hate you." His grandfather's voice was different when he spoke, and it took Jack long moments to realize why. He sounded old, for the first time in Jack's memory. He sounded like the eighty-five-year-old man that he was. And, for once, he looked tired. "I don't hate you, Jack. I miss her."

His mother, Jack knew. Laurel Endicott Sutton, the brightest light Jack had known—until now.

"I do, too, Grandfather," Jack said, his voice rough. "I always will."

"I know you do," his grandfather said in the same way, gruff and low. "I know it."

And Jack realized a great many things then, things that should have been clear to him before. He was a colossal idiot. But then, he'd known that. Everything that had happened since he'd laid eyes on Larissa Whitney five years ago told him that. But he couldn't even use her as an excuse. He had been as blind to what was happening in his relationship with his grandfather as he had been with her.

Maybe that was the Endicott curse, he thought then. This inability to see the glaring truth, the one that sat directly in the sun and shone the brightest. But he could choose not to look away. He could choose to stare directly into the glare, and see what happened.

How could he do anything less?

He reached over and put his arm over his grandfather's shoulders, noticing for the first time how frail the old man was. How much smaller than in Jack's head. He couldn't change the past, Jack thought then—the misunderstandings, the hurt pride, the nonchalant debauchery of his twenties, but he could change what came next.

And he would.

"We're going to be okay, Grandfather," he said, and he felt it ring in him like a bell. Like truth. "We're going to be fine."

Chip Van Housen would not take no for answer. Not that this was anything new.

Larissa kept her smile fastened to her face as if it had been chiseled there, and tried to pretend that she had never enjoyed anything more than Chip's decidedly lewd version of the waltz.

"You can't ignore me forever, Larissa," he said, his insipid and bloodshot eyes glued to her face. She could feel his gaze on her skin, just as she could smell the alcohol on his breath. She wondered, not for the first time, how and why she had ever spent so much of her time with this person. She had gone out of her way to do so, once upon a time. All of those memories were so dark, so blurry. Had she really hated herself that much? That seemed so hard to imagine now.

She supposed that was some kind of progress.

It was a beautiful night, crisp and bitter cold, yet deliciously warm in the cocoon of the Georgian-style mansion's courtyard, as if the gala event was claiming just a little bit of summer in the face of the long winter ahead. Lanterns and heat lamps bloomed with light and warmth, and if Larissa ignored who clutched at her on the dance floor, she might even have come close to enjoying herself.

But Chip was not one to listen, or to learn, and the third time he tried to kiss her with his loose, wet mouth, Larissa decided she'd had enough. She pulled back abruptly, shook off his hands, and simply walked away—headed for the outskirts of the party where, she could only hope, there might be fewer witnesses to what was likely to be precisely the kind of scene she wanted to avoid these days.

"You can't just walk away from me!" Chip snarled at her, catching up to her too quickly and snatching at her arm. Larissa snatched it back. She darted a look around. There was nowhere completely devoid of catty, watchful eyes—but this far corner was just cold enough, she thought, that it might provide a buffer. She could only hope.

"I just did," she said in a calm voice, completely at odds with his. "I don't want to dance with you, Chip. I was only doing it to be polite, but I'm not feeling polite anymore. Don't ask me again."

There was something handsome there in his face, in the bones, but he'd ruined it long ago. Tonight she saw only the vague suggestion of his once-boyish good looks. But a creeping meanness had taken over, and it was evident in the way his lip curled and eyes narrowed.

"You won't say no to me," he said, with a scoffing, nasty sort of laugh that made her blood chill.

"Are you sure?" she asked, an edge in her voice. "Because I think I just did."

"You don't say no, Larissa," he told her in that same awful voice. He moved in closer, his face a mask of contempt. "Ever. What game do you think you're playing? Do you really think anyone will fall for it?"

As little as Larissa had liked it when Jack had asked her similar questions, she liked it even less now. She forced her shoulders back as if she felt brave, when inside, it was as if everything had frozen solid. It was one thing to stand up to her father. But how was she supposed to stand up to the very personification of the worst of her past? She felt shame crawl over her skin, thick and greasy, but she refused to show it. She refused to let him see any part of her at all.

"Let me make this simple for you, Chip," she said, in a voice that sounded friendly on the surface, but wasn't. "You need to leave me alone. I'm not going to have a debate about it."

"You don't get to tell me what you will and won't—" he began, crowding her, using his body to try to cow her into submission. She stuck her chin in the air and refused to move.

"Stop trying to bully me," she said, her tone calm. Deliberate. It cost her. "I understand that you may not have noticed this, but I'm not the person you knew. And she's not coming back, so you're going to have find someone else to take part in all your sordid little escapades."

He stared at her for a moment, and Larissa realized, with a dawning sort of wonder, that she loathed him. That she always had. That there was no part of him that she remembered with anything but disgust. Had he always been her most effective weapon of self-destruction? How had she not realized that before? And why had she used this weak, nasty man to bludgeon herself for so long?

"This is all very inspiring, Larissa," he said, sneering. "The town whore all dressed up like someone who matters. Like a real person instead of a joke. How long do you think it will last before you end up in the nearest gutter? And who do you think is really buying it? Not one person at this party—in this city—will ever forget exactly who and what you are." He laughed that nasty laugh. "Not one."

She felt a wave of self-loathing flood her then, nearly taking her off her feet. Shame. Horror. Everything she'd tried so hard to fight. And in that moment, she knew he was right. She could see it. She felt heat on her face, at the back of her eyes, and she knew that if she looked around, they would all be laughing at her. All of them, snickering at Larissa's delusions, at her wild fantasies that she could ever be more than the tiny, worthless creature she'd always believed herself to be. That her father had told her she was. As if all the work she'd done these past weeks, and the months before, had been for nothing.

She felt her stomach hollow out, and she thought for a moment she might be sick.

But she didn't die of the shame, as perhaps she wanted to do. She breathed, her heart continued to beat, and as she stared back at Chip it occurred to her that of the two people standing there, she was the one who knew who she was. Not this lowlife, all dressed up in his black-tie costume but profoundly ugly beneath.

"Who do you think you are?" he taunted her.

And she knew in that moment that it didn't matter what Chip Van Housen—or anyone else—thought of her. She got to decide who she was. *She did.* And the shame was only powerful—could only hurt her—if she let it.

"I'm Larissa Whitney," she replied, not bothering with her stock smile, not trying to be polite, and she didn't care at all who overheard her. She was brimming with her own strength, with her own choices, and she was the one who decided what her past made her. Not Chip. Not ever. "And I don't care who you think I am."

And then she turned, sweeping away from Chip and his gaping mouth, and walked directly into Jack.

Who was standing there as if he'd been there for some time.

As if he'd heard every horrible word.

CHAPTER TWELVE

LARISSA wanted to die, right there and then.

She wanted to be sucked down into the bowels of New York City and left there to rot—anything but this. Anything but staring in horror at the man she loved, the man whose good opinion meant more to her than anything else in the world or in her life, with Chip's words ringing in the air all around them. Polluting everything.

All that strength and power seemed to contract inside of her, and she had to suck in a breath to keep the sudden dizziness from sending her to her knees. He reached out a hand and took her arm, his palm so warm, so perfect against her skin, and she felt a sea of regret pull her under then, fierce and unfightable, and there was nothing she could do but look at him. At that beautiful face, beloved by so many. At those bittersweet-chocolate eyes that saw too much and not enough, and at that lush, dangerous mouth that could tease her into ecstasy and tear her into pieces.

What was the point of changing her whole life—of vanquishing her father and seizing control of all that was hers—if she still couldn't have this man? If he thought the very worst of her and could have it confirmed on a random Friday night in December, unsolicited and unprovoked, from the vilest of sources? She felt contaminated by her own history.

She wanted to die, but she didn't. She never did. And so she had no choice but to look Jack in the eye and try not to dissolve into tears. If she couldn't have what she wanted more than anything else, she might as well attempt to hang on to some shred of her dignity.

"It looks like you were right about me after all," she said, and she couldn't manage to make her voice light. She forced a smile instead, though it felt more like a grimace. "You must feel so vindicated."

He did not react for a long moment, staring down at her as if he was trying to translate her words, break the code, figure her out. As if she was written in hieroglyphics and he could not begin to imagine the meaning of each shape in the stone. Something passed over his face, through his eyes and then was gone.

He looked over her shoulder at Chip, and his fingers tightened slightly against the bare skin of her upper arm, making goose bumps rise, making her fight off a shiver. Then he returned his gaze to hers, dark and determined. And smiled. A bright, happy smile. Charming. Delicious.

"Dance with me," he said.

Of all the things she'd imagined he might have said, that was not on the list. She blinked at him, trying to process his words as well as that devastating, surprising smile.

"Dance?" she echoed.

"I know you know how," he said, in that way of his that called to mind his golden, summer self, outshining all the rest of them on all those New England beaches. It made her chest feel tight. It made heads turn, seeking out all that light, all that sun, in the middle of a chilly winter night. "I've seen you do it."

"With you?" She felt thick and simultaneously too light. Feverish. She thought perhaps she should go lie down in a quiet corner somewhere and wait for morning. Or perhaps for next year. But she couldn't seem to bring herself to move.

"I'm an excellent dancer, Larissa," he said, still in full *Jack Endicott Sutton* mode. He was dazzling. And he was drawing ever more attention as he spoke. "My grandfather would have it no other way."

And then it clicked, finally. Larissa felt something like relief—and something much sharper, much more damaging—slice through her then, making her feel that she could breathe. Or anyway, understand. He was doing this deliberately. It was a far greater repudiation of Chip to treat her like someone worthy of the famous Jack Sutton charm than it was to slap back at the other man.

Larissa just couldn't understand why he would bother.

She let him draw her with him toward the dance floor and then let him pull her into his arms. She felt too hot and then too cold, as if a volcano was set to erupt beneath her skin. As if the ground beneath them was buckling and heaving. She looked at him and the world seemed to spin too fast all around her, and she had to look away to keep her balance.

She saw all the grand families of New York City arrayed around the courtyard. All that Knickerbocker and Gilded Age gentility, Upper Ten Thousand denizens, robber barons and railway tycoons, New England blue bloods, and the infusion, here and there yet never talked about in good company, of new money or Hollywood glamour. She and Jack were made of this place, these people. And yet she found herself yearning with all of her battered soul for that grand old house on a lonely hill, hidden away on a desolate island, where they had been so close to whomever they'd wanted to be, for a little while. Just a little while, but she still told herself it mattered.

She rested one hand on his strong shoulder, and let him close the other in his as he led her around the floor in an easy, perfectly executed waltz. The heat of his other palm seemed to burn into the small of her back, branding her. Making her flush anew with the heat that was always, only, his. Her body felt too alive, too sensitive. Too aware. And yet she could still feel the echo of Chip's words like a film over her skin, making her feel dirty and desperate. It almost hurt to be so close to Jack, and know that, in reality, she'd never been further away from him.

She did not have to be told that this would be the last time they touched. It made sense, now, to look back at the other night and recognize that it had been their goodbye. He had never lied to her, had he? He had been completely up front about what was expected of him and why he would do as he was told. His duty. She even admired him for it, on some level.

Even as it crushed her.

"It's nice of you to do this," she said, unable even to pretend to smile. She fixed her gaze at some point over his shoulder, and forced herself to keep her chin in the air, her eyes clear and dry. "I had no idea your charitable intentions cast so wide a net. We fallen women of New York High Society salute you."

He turned his head and caught her gaze, and she

swallowed, hard. Her stomach flipped. His mouth was too close and there was a certain kindness in those bittersweet depths—and it broke her heart all over again.

"What do you think is happening here?" he asked mildly. Almost indulgently.

"I have no idea." Her tongue was turning to ash in her mouth. Why was he doing this to her? Why was he prolonging the agony?

"Use that magnificent brain of yours, Larissa," he suggested. "The one, I am reliably informed, that you used to outsmart your father just yesterday."

She was pleased he knew. Too pleased. Reality reasserted itself, unpleasantly, and she looked away again.

"I can't play these games with you, Jack," she said quietly. "You should not let your grandfather see you with me. There are, no doubt, a flock of appropriate young heiresses happy to fight over you. I can see at least five of them by the bar."

He pulled her closer, too close and yet not close enough, never close enough and never again—but she could not seem to do anything but fall into his gaze again when he looked at her, into her.

"I don't want them," he said. Softly. Deliberately. "I want you."

* * *

"You do not," she said, her voice something like affronted. It would have made him laugh, had he not seen the darkness that lurked in her gaze.

"I have already proven it," he said. "Over and over again. I'm crushed that you haven't been paying attention."

"You're talking about sex," she said, and there was a crack in her voice. "Because what else could you possibly be talking about?"

The dullness in her tone made him feel violent. He wanted to find that Van Housen creature again and put a fist through his pretty, dissipated face. But he restrained himself.

"Why would you listen to anything that—" he began.

"I haven't listened to Chip Van Housen in years, if ever," she said, cutting him off. Her eyes shimmered in the lights from the winter lanterns, and the green in them glowed. Her lips crooked into something wry and painful. "But I listened to you."

He could hear his own voice, lashing into her, tearing strips off her, and for what? To make himself feel better that he couldn't seem to let go of her? That she'd haunted him for so many years? What did that make him?

"Larissa…" He whispered her name.

"You hate me," she said, her voice clear. Direct.

Just like that damning green gaze. "You think I'm a worthless whore."

That sat between them, carried on the sweet notes from the band, batted into the air and showering back down over them like the lights from above. And suddenly, he saw the whole of their time in Maine as if through a different lens. A different view. Hers.

Because if Larissa had been telling the truth about herself, about why she had turned up there, about everything—and Jack admitted to himself that it had been quite some time since he'd truly doubted her, no matter what he might have said— if all of that was true, it made him the greatest bastard of all time.

He stared down at her, at the stark pain that he could see etched so clearly into her face, her eyes. He could not imagine why she was even here, looking at him like this, holding him as if there was some part of her that didn't detest him as she should.

"I do not hate you," he said, the words coming from a place inside him he wasn't sure he'd ever accessed before, except in grief. "I love you."

He wasn't sure what he'd expected. A choir? The band to swell into a chorus?

But something like temper moved over her face, and she only blinked.

"How nice," she murmured, with acid insincerity. "That, of course, fixes everything. It's the adult version of calling a do-over, really. I'll just pretend that nothing that happened between us actually happened—"

He wasn't sure if he'd stopped moving before, or if he stopped then. But he couldn't keep up the farce of dancing when she was this close to slipping away from him. All over again, and for good this time. He couldn't bring himself to care about any of the people around them, his grandfather— none of it. Larissa was the only person who had mattered to him in longer than he could remember.

He let his hands move to her hips, anchoring her in front of him, as if she might try to run for the street.

"I am an ass," he said, distinctly. She sucked in a shocked sort of breath. But she didn't pull away. "You are the only woman who has ever gotten to me."

"The only one who walked away from you, you mean," she interjected.

"Repeatedly," he agreed. He searched her face. "And still I can't stay away from you. I can't bear to be apart from you. I think I've been in love with you since we met at that party more than five years ago."

"You wouldn't know love if it bit you!" she hissed at him, but he could see the storm gathering in her, dark and wild, like the rains that swept across his beloved island, and that cold, hard knot in his solar plexus began to ease.

"Then why don't you bite me, Larissa, and see what happens," he suggested. She flushed, and he felt that fear loosen even more. He took her hands in his, pulling them up to his chest. Holding her gaze, he kissed each one. "I love you. I do. I don't know how to prove it to you, but I will. Give me the chance, and I will. I promise."

She stared at him. Hours might have passed. Days. She let out a long breath, and then she started and looked around them. They were standing in the center of the dance floor, in the middle of one of the biggest parties of the year. They were not exactly hidden. If he was worried about being seen with her, it was clearly already too late. He could see the speculation, hear the murmurs. No doubt, she could, too. She reddened slightly, and looked back at him.

"You are making a scene," she hissed at him, but there was something else in her eyes. Something he recognized. The truth of Larissa Whitney, the one, he thought with satisfaction, that only he knew.

"I don't care," he replied.

And she smiled. Not that mysterious, calculated smile that she used as her armor, but something real. It was beautiful and rare, and it lit up her face, and him and the whole of Manhattan. It made him feel like flying. It made him think he already was.

"You say that now," she teased him. "But you haven't experienced the true joy of being the focus of so many evil New York City gossips in some time, have you?"

"Then we'd better give them something to talk about," he said. He took her in his arms again, dipped her to hear a delighted peal of laughter pour from her like the sweetest, purest bell, and then, at last, in full view of Manhattan's finest and wealthiest, he kissed her.

The new year was still in its infancy and they moved together in the wide bed, tucked up on the second floor of Scatteree Pines while a snowstorm swirled against the bay windows outside. Inside, they were safe and warm. Hot, as they teased each other with their mouths, hands, bodies.

Larissa had never felt like this—so much, so bright, nothing hidden. Jack moved inside her, around her, and she clung to him and found herself made new with every thrust, every slide of skin against skin, every time they fell over the edge of the world together.

"I love you," she murmured drowsily against his perfect chest much later, while the snow still spiraled down from the dark sky and the wind howled over the lonely hill, cocooning them on this desolate island together. Just where she wanted to stay. She smiled against his skin, his heartbeat beneath her cheek.

His hand moved lazily down her back, and she arched slightly against it, boneless and replete.

"You'll have to marry me," he said, as if he'd given the matter a great deal of thought. As if there had been some debate.

Perhaps there had been—but not, Larissa thought, recently. They were too much the same. From the very same world, even possessed of the same kind of pasts. So there was only the future for them, clear and golden. She had no doubt.

"Only if you promise me one thing," she said, shifting against him so she could look up at him, his dark brown eyes still bright with passion as he gazed back at her.

"Anything," he said, his voice a rasp in the shadowed room, a rumble beneath her. Oh, this man. This impossible, maddening, perfect man. She'd had no idea it was even possible to love this much. And she'd never had another person love her so absolutely. So wholly. As if she had never been ruined at all. As if she was brand-new and squeaky clean, inside and out.

The longer he loved her, the more she thought she might just believe it, after all.

"I want only the most deadly dull society affair," she said, smiling at him. "The full, traditional spectacle. Every recognizable name in New York. Rockefellers and Roosevelts. A five-mile train and six dozen handpicked bridesmaids with perfect pedigrees."

Jack laughed. "Why would you want such a thing?" he asked. "It sounds like a nightmare. Your nightmare, to be precise. And, let me assure you, mine."

"I don't want there to be any doubt," she said, tracing a finger over his delicious mouth. "I don't want anyone to think that this is a mistake, or that I somehow tricked you into this with my evil wiles."

"But you did," he said, pulling her finger into his mouth to suck at it for a searingly hot moment, and then bringing her face to his, and kissing her. "You did it years ago, and I've been at a loss ever since."

Larissa smiled against his mouth. "I want to treat it the way the rest of them do, the way your grandfather always wanted you to do. A great and financially sound merger of two storied American families, as expected since our births."

"That doesn't sound like you at all," he said, framing her face with his hands, his eyes searching hers. "I want to marry *you*, Larissa. Not some fantasy version of you, tidied up for wider consumption."

He meant that, she thought, with a wonder that

only grew, and never seemed to dull. He truly meant that.

"It will be our wedding gift to our families," she told him. She leaned over the side of the bed, and rummaged around until she found what she was looking for. Holding the handcuffs in her hand, she rolled back to Jack, and smiled.

A real smile. Wicked, but real.

"But the marriage…" she whispered. She crawled over him to clip one strong wrist to the iron headboard. She let her hands smooth their way back down his chest, and straddled him, making him groan as he hardened against her once more. "The marriage is just for us," she said, and rolled her hips to take him deep inside herself.

She set an easy, unhurried pace, and he met it, his eyes bright on hers. And that electric kick of heat burst into flame again, immolation and celebration, all of it theirs. Jack pulled against the handcuff, letting it clank loudly against the iron. He laughed when she stopped moving, her hands braced on his abdomen as she stared down at him, as if she expected him to complain.

"I told you," he said. "There's nothing you've done that I haven't done first. You can't shock me, Larissa, no matter what you do." His smile was crooked and sweet, golden like the sun, and all hers. She believed him. His dark brows rose in challenge. Daring her. His eyes loved her—all of her. "But you can always try."

And so she did.

* * * * *